Strings

HARD ROCK HARLOTS
BOOK ONE

by

KENDALL GREY

Published by
Howling Mad Press, LLC
P.O. Box 660
Bethlehem, GA 30620
United States of America
howlingmadpress.com

Edited by Jennifer Sommersby Young
Cover by QDesign
Stock purchased from DepositPhotos, ©johan-jk

ISBN 10: 1-947830-04-X
ISBN 13: 978-1-947830-04-2

Manufactured in the United States of America
First Paperback Edition: June 2013

DEDICATION

This book belongs to the readers who believed in me and to all the artists who make the world a beautiful, better place.

May the strings that bind us never break
May our wild asses forever shake
May our unquenchable fire keep our dreams awake

MY BOYFRIEND LEFT ME FOR JESUS

Twenty-five years ago today, I exited my mama's womb center stage and stormed Planet Earth, guns blazing, taking no prisoners. Crashes of lightning and thunder announced my birth. A cyclone killed nearly 600 people in Bangladesh and left half a million homeless. I'm not saying I had anything to do with that shit, but when a force like mine is born, the Universe takes notice. Cause and effect. Yin and yang. Pomp and circumstance.

Mom says I screamed nonstop for an hour after she squirted me out. I've taken a few breaks to catch my breath since, but for the most part, I'm still screaming today.

My name is Letty Dillinger, and I was born to rock your face off.

If you come to one of my shows, you'll leave either wanting to *be* me or wanting to *do* me.

My music has that effect on people. Or it *will* once I bust out of these shackles of banality and show the world what I'm made of.

I'm the lead singer and bass player for an all-chick, '70s-style rock band, Cherry Buzz Float. Yeah, the name's a little lame, but guys like cherries and buzzes and tits that float on the water.

Me and my bandmates play up the bad-girl attitude to appeal to our audience, but I'm not really that pretentious. For me, life is about the music. That amazing ride you catch when the notes and rhythms snap into place, and you connect with the human beings involved in shaping audio beauty.

As much as I love the orgasms my bass gives me when I sit on the monitor and hit a low C, music is even better when *people* jump into the fray of physics and take it to a higher level.

Music is about my drummer Jinx—the female version of John Fucking Bonham on crack—beating the shit out of her skins in perfect sync with my bass vibrating the walls like an earthquake.

Music is about fishing for the right notes to match Kate's awesome guitar riffs and complementing her screaming highs with my window-rattling lows.

Music is about freeing the lyrics my heart holds dear and watching meaning root, blossom, and spread like a virus across our fans' faces.

Music is about The Rock, the roll, and the crazy shit that comes with the territory.

At least when I'm onstage, it is.

Real life is a lot less glamorous. I only play live a couple times a month these days. The band's not really moving in the direction I'd like it to, and I sure as shit ain't making any cash playing frat parties for drunk, rich squids.

Fuckin' dreams. Who needs 'em?

I live in Athens, Georgia. It's December 1. Cold as a witch's tit in a brass bra. The college kids are wrapping up fall semester and heading home soon. Trixies, squids, and townies troll downtown, drunk and looking for temporary love when they should be banging their books at the library. I glance wistfully out the window from my barstool perch. Instead of raising hell with my friends, I'm sitting alone at BAR-k, the bar whose clever name salutes the local football team (go Dawgs!), on my birthday, wondering where my life went wrong.

"Why the long face?" Bartender Rob tosses a stained white towel over his shoulder and leans across the nicked wood. He rests his meaty elbows in a puddle of liquor leftovers. I eye the spot and manage to keep my tongue in my mouth.

No licking the bar. You're not drunk enough. Yet.

I do love me some booze, and I'm living off the coins I found in my couch cushions until payday. With a calloused index finger, I stir my vodka martini—the one birthday present I allowed my broke-ass self to buy.

"The short version? My boyfriend left me for Jesus. I'm stuck in a dead-end waitressing job, clogging people's arteries at Fat Johnny's Barbeque Shack, making jack shit. I'm earning even less busting ass at the gig I *want* to be doing."

The part about my boyfriend is a white lie. He's really just a guy I was bonking for a while. Technicality. But the rest is one hundred percent truth.

"No one gives a mangy monkey boner about *art* anymore. Nothing but a bunch of zero-talent sellouts in this fucking town." I meet Rob's eyes. "Man, I'm twenty-five today, and I have nothing to show for it."

Rob straightens. "My mama always said, 'If you can't beat 'em, join 'em.'"

I shake my head. "Fuck that. I'd rather starve than sell out."

Yeah, I'm a little rabid about this particular stick-to-your-guns philosophy. Some people find strength in religion. I believe in music, and I defend it with everything I've got, even when things don't go my way.

I played the unfortunate role of a human pinball paddled back and forth between my divorced parents for most of my life. In my darkest moments, solace and light came from listening to my mom's '70s cassette tapes. For a few years, music was my only friend. Nobody else understood me. It helped me through the rough patches and gave me motivation to pick up the bass at fourteen.

Even though I haven't made it yet, music is still the one thing that keeps me steady and sane. You don't fuck with shit that does you right. Especially when it's all you've got.

I just wish ...

If wishes were horses, beggars would ride.

"Happy fucking birthday," Rob says.

"Yeah, cheers, asshole." I raise my glass and swallow the whole drink in three big gulps. Rob snickers and wanders over to a customer waving bills at him from the register.

The guy one seat away from me laughs, so I glance at him. He's hunched over the bar like he's guarding his drink, with his head turned toward me. Five o' clock shadow, pierced eyebrow, dark brown fauxhawk, plugs in his earlobes—not too big, though. He wears a black wool pea coat-looking thing, jeans, and a pair of dark sunglasses.

"Something funny, Shades?" I ask.

"Your boyfriend leaving you for Jesus." He has kind of a gruff voice. His face is okay, but it's hard to tell what he really looks like with those glasses covering his most important features. I like his hands, though. They're rough like mine.

"I knew something was wrong with him when he complained about me asking for anal. What guy doesn't want anal?" I twirl my empty glass by its long stem. "He was kind of a dick trickle, so it's not like I miss him or anything. Though the sex was decent. Better than my current prospects."

Damn, I'm dying for another drink. Maybe just one more. I'm pretty sure I got a couple bucks stuffed in my car's ashtray for emergencies. I shoot a bird at Rob, who nods.

"Definitely something wrong with a guy who doesn't want to sodomize his woman." Shades takes a sip from his glass. A wrist tattoo peeks out from his coat sleeve. I can't tell what it is.

"Nah, I wanted to sodomize *him*. He wasn't on board with the plan. That's when the Holier Than Thou shit started. 'Jesus doesn't approve of butt-fucking.' Jesus this. Jesus that. What the hell, man? Don't you think Jesus would want you to be happy? How will you ever be happy if you don't try new things? Christ, it's just a dildo up the ass. Loosen the fuck up."

Shades chokes on his drink, wipes his mouth with a coat sleeve, and laughs. Gorgeous teeth.

A glass slides across the bar from Rob a few feet away. I stop it with my open hand and smile.

Rob grins and saunters over. "I got you this Flaming Armadillo for your birthday, my dear. I hope it fits." He flicks his lighter and ignites the liquid in the glass. Blue flames dance. I salivate.

"Rob, it's perfect. You shouldn't have."

"You're welcome."

I pick up the shot and blow it out. *To another year of dream chasing. Maybe this'll be the one where I finally make it big.* "Happy birthday to me."

Gulp. Down the chute it goes, and I lose five IQ points as the alcohol gets busy with my already precarious brain chemistry. At least somebody's getting some action.

Shades raises his glass and shoots whatever he's drinking. "Did you make a wish?"

I'm not telling my real wish. That shit won't come true if you spill it. Instead, I say, "All I want for my birthday is to get fucked unconscious with no strings attached." Not a lie.

"What a coincidence. I've got a big dick, a bar tab, and the local cab company's number on speed dial." The guy's eyes bore into me from behind the dark lenses, and I have a momentary lapse in vaginal secretion control.

Clean up on aisle twelve, stat!

His pierced eyebrow arches, his lips part to reveal an orthodontist's magnum opus, and Shades suddenly looks pretty fucking hot.

I know it's the alcohol and my raging libido ganging up on me. I know tomorrow morning, this motherfucker is gonna turn out to be the ugliest fucking turd a worm-infested dog ever shat. I know it's the insecurities from my professional life urging me to take unwarranted risks in my personal life. But by God, if I don't get laid tonight, my cooter will go nuclear and wipe out a city block.

Nobody wants that.

I face the guy full on and wave him into the empty stool between us. My brain sloshes every time I move my head. Shades scoots over, leaving his empty glass behind. Now that he's closer, I take a good look at him. Mostly clean. Fingernails are free of dirt. Smells nice.

"What's your name, pussycat?" he says.

I glance down at his lap in hopes of catching a hint of this Woodrow he's so damn proud of. Too dark to see anything, so I lay a hand on his thigh. "Now why would you want to go and complicate shit by asking my name? Just call me Lucky. 'Cause you're getting Lucky tonight, Shades."

Yeah, I said that. I guess this means I'm committed. I really hope the dick comes through for me. I stretch my hand up a little higher and brush … oh yeah, there it is. Plumped halfway down his thigh and more stubborn than me.

Happy birthday, indeed.

"Okay, Lucky. It's you, me, a trip to the adult toy store, and a hotel." He pulls out his wallet and tosses a hundred-dollar bill on the bar. Shit, he wasn't kidding. About anything.

Rob heads over. He can smell big money a mile away.

"Give me a bottle of tequila. To go." Shades stands up and readjusts his boner.

As they negotiate the terms of the hostage tequila's release, I watch this dude. He's taller than me—who isn't?—and has a laid-back, old-school vibe about him despite the modern tattoos and piercings. I like it. He must be as desperate as I am to get laid, otherwise he wouldn't be jerking off Ben Franklin for a bottle of cheap tequila and an even cheaper date.

I stand, and the floor tilts left. I grab the back of the barstool. Oh yeah, this is gonna be some fun shit. Halfway in the bag already, and I have some guy I never met taking me out for drinks and dildos.

But you know what? It's my birthday, and I'm horny as a teenager discovering Internet porn. I'll never see this asshole again. Fuck it.

Shades tucks the brown-wrapped bottle under his arm and faces me. Still with the glasses, yet now I'm kinda grateful for them. Once my shameless shame is complete, I want to remember as little of his face as possible.

"Ready to rock, Lucky?"

I snort. "I was born ready."

Rob salutes me behind him. "Have fun."

"Oh, I will." And out the door I go with a man I hope will have me living up to my new name in about ten minutes.

PUSSY GRENADES AND ASS BUNKERS

"You always pick up strangers for sex?" Shades says as we head down the street. His breath curls in a wisp with the cold air. Damn, he's a *lot* taller than me.

Slosh, slosh. And damn, I'm druuunk. "Do you?"

"They usually throw themselves at me. I have to beat them off."

"I'd like to beat you off." I giggle. Yeah, I said that too. "You got condoms?" Best to get business out of the way so we can enjoy the pleasure.

"I'll pick some up at the adult store."

I stop. "You're serious about that?"

"What? You bumming me with a strap-on?" He shrugs. "Sure."

What have I gotten myself into? "You're gay."

He snickers. "No."

"Bi."

"Open-minded."

Well, ain't this the shit? I was totally fucking joking, but now that he's game, I kinda am too. "You ever been butt-boinked by a drunk, dildo-clad woman before?"

There's that naughty grin again. "No, but I'll try anything once."

Oh, I like this guy. He's the total opposite of that uptight asshole I was fucking before. And now that we're out of the shitty bar light, he looks even better.

Probably the tequila goggles.

Fuck it.

"You got any diseases I need to be worried about?"

"Other than an acute case of blue balls? No."

I look him square in the glasses. No signs of twitchiness. No oozing mouth sores. Breath is good. This guy's cleared for landing. "Okay. Let's go."

A million other questions rush through my drunk head, but with the most important ones out of the way, I keep quiet. Besides, the more I know about him, the more I'll *want* to know, and I can't get involved with anyone right now. I have other things to focus on, like becoming famous.

"I'm gonna need a strap-on, a dildo, some lube, condoms, and more of that tequila."

He hands me the bottle, which I open and chug while blocking the entire sidewalk. A guy with a stick up his ass walks by and says, "You can't drink on the street. It's against the law."

I scowl at the party pooper and turn my face to the half-moon winking at me from above. "Fuck your drinking laws, Athens, Georgia. I'm invincible!"

Shades laughs, swipes the bottle, and pulls a hearty swig too. A little of the liquor spills from the corner of his mouth, and I pull his head down by the ears to lick it. I get a whiff of his cologne, and my head spins faster.

Flashing a white-toothed rock-star smile, he recaps the glass. A trio of bodacious sorority girls stumbles past, and he doesn't even glance. I'm all his? Aww, shucks.

The bottle goes into the bag, and Shades leads me by the arm to a parked cab on the corner. We tumble into the back seat, a mess of arms and legs and foggy tequila breath. A hand falls on my boob and squeezes. If my nipples could ejaculate, they would. God, this is happening so fast, and I'm *so* horny. I fumble in the dark until I find his hard cock, and I stroke him. He tells the driver where we're going, and I drop my head into his lap.

Fuck, this is a big dick. My cooch produces another juice explosion as I slide my teeth along the torpedo testing the strength of his jeans. He adjusts in the seat, grabs a fistful of my long, fire-engine-red hair, and guides my mouth with expert precision. He's done this before. I imagine twisting my locks around his dick like a cock ring and sucking the head until he comes all over my face. Or in my mouth. Or on my tits.

I do love the cock, no matter which way it comes.

And I'm fucked up on tequila, which makes me not just horny but also invincible, as I mentioned to Athens, Georgia, moments ago.

Shades sucks in a quick breath and tightens his grip. Shit, I must've gotten a little excited and nipped him. Pushing the mess of hair from my face, I sit up. I assume his eyes are on me. Wish I could see them. I sure as fuck can't read his expression with those damn glasses in the way.

Nope. Resist the temptation, Letty. Fuck him like a Roman nympho whore with a flaming crotch, let him put it out with a cum spritzer, then run like hell.

He leans in as if to kiss me but doesn't follow through. The fucking tease. My nipples harden to stones as I fantasize about him licking, sucking, biting one. His hands encircle my waist, and before my drunk ass registers a hint of impishness, one of them is skidding down my butt crack on a crash course with the liquid gold erupting from Mount Vagina. Two fingers on a mission bypass my asshole and surprise attack my primed pussy from behind. Like a ninja *boss!*

I gasp—not from the shock, but from the unexpected pleasure. Grinning like he owns me—which I'll admit, he totally does—he slides in and out.

The pressure builds too fast. Jesus Christ. I'm gonna come in the back of a taxi while a guy I don't know fingers me on our way to pick up a strap-on from a sex toy store.

I yank his arm from behind me and shove one of his Letty-drizzled fingers into his mouth. He makes a show of licking me off him, which gets me wetter. I smile and snag a lick of my own, skidding my tongue slowly up the digits until I reach the calloused pad of his middle finger. Here's where I show him what his dick is missing.

Long pulls on the sensitive tip of his finger, then spirals up and down the length drag a heavy exhale out of him. I maintain a steady vacuum as I lick the underside, wishing it were his shaft twitching in my mouth. God, I want to taste him.

I ruffle his cute hair and whisper in his ear, "Your cock is next."

His smile widens, grabs me by the pussy, and diddles.

I'm seriously melting, despite the cold. And sorely tempted to mount this motherfucker here and now for an appetizer in preparation for the upcoming main course. If I don't get release soon—

The car rolls to a stop in a parking lot. "This the place?" the cabbie says.

I'm grateful for the interruption because my twat is so wet, I'll be leaving a tip in this guy's taxi in the form of a monstrous cum stain. How the hell do you get goose juice out of a car's upholstery? His problem. Not mine.

"I'll be back in a minute." Shades pushes the liquor bottle into my hands, gropes my tit again, and kisses me hard. The scratch of his rough stubble against my smooth cheek cocks the loaded round of cum shots eagerly awaiting detonation in my pussy.

In a flash, he's gone. Seconds later, I miss him already. There's nothing else to do but drink more tequila. So, I slide down the seat where the driver can't see me in the rearview, and I imbibe.

Here's the thing about me and tequila. We're tight. I know exactly how it'll affect me and at what point I should slap its ass and send it home. I've already passed stages one and two: "I'm Rich," and "I'm Good Looking." Stage three, "I'm Bulletproof," is imminent. I tip up the bottle for another shot.

Oh hell, who am I kidding? I'm totally in stage three. My goal tonight is to maintain a steady stream of invincibility. If I hit stage four—"I'm Invisible"—I'll likely pass out, and that would ruin all my fun.

I can't see anything in the dark, but the bottle feels kinda light already. Maybe I should take off my shirt and pour the rest down my front so Shades can lick it off.

Body shots.

Nipple shots.

Pussy shots!

I clutch the bottle to my chest. I'm *so* saving this for later.

The driver lifts his chin and peers at me in the rearview. He wants me. I can tell.

The door pops open, and a welcome rush of cold air stings my face. "Shades, baby!" I throw my arms around his shoulders and sloppy-drunk lick his stubble. That pierced eyebrow hitches again. He drops a brown paper bag between his feet on the floorboard. I can't fucking wait to see what he got. The door slams shut.

I lean close and whisper in his ear, "The driver wants to have sex with me. He's staring at my tits."

"Can't have that. Those belong to me." His hand worms its way up the back of my shirt. With one flick of the wrist, my bra clasp pops and unleashes The Girls.

"Where to?" the driver says. He's salivating. I know it.

I wipe the corner of my mouth. Damn, I am too.

"Armstrong Suites downtown." Rough fingers pinch and tweak my nipples. His palm kneads my aching cans. Jesus, if he keeps that up, I'll have a titgasm.

Hold on. "Armstrong Suites? The new hotel chain? Isn't that place ridiculously expensive?"

Shades removes his hand, smiles, and notches his glasses down just enough for me to see the mischief in his eyes. "Only the best for Lucky."

13

Great. This guy's gonna fuck me, slice me up, and sell my pieces for turtle soup or some shit.

"Are you a serial killer?" Did I say that out loud?

The driver raises a brow. Shades laughs. "Only if you want me to be."

I think the cabbie might be a serial killer.

I snuggle against Shades's side. He opens his pea coat—who wears shit like this besides homeless people?—and I tug it around my arms. God, I can really smell him now, and he's fucking amazing. Like ginger, pepper, pine, and musk all mixed together. I don't know jack shit about men's perfume, but whatever he's wearing punches my hormones in the nuts and holds my impulse control for ransom.

I no longer care if Shades is a homeless serial killer. I just want to fuck his brains out. He can do whatever he wants afterward.

Yeah.

I spend the rest of the drive trying to convince my famished beaver that dinner is coming soon. *Patience, Gertrude. Patience.* Seriously, this bitch needs her own personal air conditioning unit. Maybe an adult diaper.

Dribble, dribble.

Finally. The cabbie parks in front of the fancy hotel I normally sneer at every time I drive past. Places like this are for snobby, rich bitches. Being a scumbag rocker lends itself more to sleeping in cars and dilapidated vans than the sophistication of even a one-star roach motel. Shit like the Armstrong Suites? This is the closest I'll probably ever get to fame.

Shades pays the serial killer, and I follow my "date" out. Once on the blacktop, I wobble and look down at my badass combat boots. Still badass.

I sneak a glance back inside to see if I really did leave a wet spot on the seat. Holy shit, I did! I'm so proud of myself. "Take care," I call to the driver and flip him off as he speeds away.

Outside the main entrance, Shades faces me. His hidden gaze sears a trail down to my open coat and the recently liberated medium-sized knockers begging to play Got Your Nosey with his face. His body is big, his stance tight as a wire. He's both intimidating and sexy as hell.

I get an anxious feeling, like I want to know everything about him so I can stalk him later, but the stupid voice of reason cuts through the tequila haze and hammers my big toe with a thunderous NO!

Fuck and get out of there. You cannot see this asshole again. Go fucking wild.

Yeah. That's the plan.

"You ready to meet God?" I ask, bold as balls on the outside but quivering like newborn fawn legs on the inside.

"I *am* God."

I believe him.

Gush-o-rama.

He steps close, yanks my hips to his cock, and strokes me in front of the whole wide world. Okay, maybe our coats give us some cover, but anyone paying attention can totally see he's got me by the crotch. Surely, he feels how wet I am. My jeans are a hot mess, and my drunk ass wants this guy way too much.

"And as the Supreme Creator of the Universe, I grant you permission to do whatever dark, unholy sexual acts you want for your birthday—"

I bounce on the balls of my feet and clap like a little girl.

"—*provided* when it's *my* birthday, I get to perform upon your person whatever dark, unholy sexual acts *I* desire."

I clench my thighs together to keep from pressure washing the pavement.

"Sounds fair enough." *Considering I'll never see you again.*

15

"You've got yourself a deal, Shades."

Could this night get any better?

I glance to the hotel. Why, yes. Yes, I think it can.

He wiggles his finger in the valley of my cunt. Another wave of wetness seeps through my jeans. Holding my stare—at least I think he is—he pops the finger in his mouth and blatantly enjoys it.

That's it. I can't take any more. I drag him toward the entrance.

White twinkling lights decorate the small trees planted around the lot. My guess is they're not there to pay homage to the holiday season. These are business-as-usual lights. Inside is where Father Christmas ate too many cranberries and broccoli and shat a storm of red and green across every available surface. Yet, somehow the product of Santa's colitis is classy and fragrant.

I wait by the elevator while Shades pays for the room. Damn, I need more tequila. The buzz is waning. I tap my foot to the bass line of the song playing in my head, hoping it'll hurry shit along. Music is the only thing in my life that calms me, and I need a three-hour symphony right now.

When Shades strides around the corner, everything flips to slow motion. We get in the elevator. He pushes me against the mirrored wall inside, forcing my arms to the glass and holding them tightly. His mouth crashes into mine—raw, starved, intent. I rally against him but can't budge. Another surge of heat waters my nether bush. He presses his hard cock into the cradle of my hips, and I grind against it as his mouth claims me in a long, lingering, intense kiss. I give up fighting. What's the point?

I lick his bottom lip and then bite it. The motherfucker love-taps my face. I slap him back. He straightens, flexes his muscles, making himself look bigger, like a horny peacock with something to prove. I clutch his rocks and twist so hard, his face turns red.

The doors slide open, and I guide him backward out of the box by the balls. "Where to, lover?"

With a pussy-tickling laugh, he scoops me up and throws me over his shoulder like a sack of dog food. I squeal and kick. I smack his ass and then poke his butthole through his jeans with my thumb. He never breaks his stride. Dude has me exactly where he wants me.

He sets me down before the last door at the end of the long corridor. It's a corner room. Key goes in, door opens, lights switch on, and I nearly shit myself. With my jaw hanging and swinging in the breeze, I wander inside, turn in a circle to take it all in. Jesus jamming with a giraffe, this place is monstrous. I trot through the suite on a discovery mission.

Kitchen, living area, king-sized bed, huge bathroom with a hot tub. The hotel "room" is bigger than my entire apartment. I turn to Shades. "You really are gonna kill me, aren't you?"

His lopsided grin triggers another eruption of twat lava. He sits on the edge of the bed and reaches for his sunglasses.

I stop him. "Leave them on. I like them." *Need* them would be the more accurate phrasing, but he doesn't need to know my reasons.

He stares at me. At least, I think he's staring.

Uncomfortable with his scrutiny, I unlace my boots and punt them aside. Wriggle out of my coat and toss it to the floor. Grab the tequila and down a long swig, wincing as the burn ignites my throat. I set the liquor on a bedside table. With my back to him, I slowly pull my shirt up and over my head. Lose the dangling bra. Cover The Girls coyly with my arms. Turn and blow him a kiss.

His dick is so hard, I can see its outline from here. I snatch the bottle up and tease my nipples to attention with the butt end of the glass. My other hand disappears down the front of my jeans, and I finger myself. I swirl my passion fruit juice over a nipple until it's shiny. Shades shoots off the bed and latches on.

He's all fucking man. Heat. Urgency. Demand. He bites my nipple, teases it with his teeth and tongue, driving me to the edge of madness. My head tilts up to the ceiling, and I clutch him harder to my tit. Hot, hurried breath. Those fucking glasses cold on my skin. He yanks my pants down, and the snap protests with a loud pop. I barely get off the next heartbeat before his tongue is on my clit.

So glad I shaved down there today.

He flicks my hood hard and fast. A pair of fingers gets involved, and I hook a leg around his neck. This is hotter than any cunnilingus I've ever been a recipient of, and I've had a hot lesbian stripper go down on me. Believe me, those bitches know how to lick a cunt. But Shades is even better. Like he's got an extra appendage or some shit.

I look down. Fucking Jesus, it's pierced. His tongue is pierced. How did I not notice before?

That's all she wrote. I watch the ball of his silver stud going to work, beating on my little bald girl in her boat. I hiss through clenched teeth as an orgasm hits me so hard, I lose my balance.

But I don't fall. Shades has been holding me up the whole time, arms like metal bands wrapped around my thigh and supporting my ass. He refuses to stop, despite the climax. I shove his head away. He goes down on his back with a pleased grin, and I drop on top of him.

Enough of this, I need some dick and another orgasm to go.

Shades wears way too many clothes for a drunk, horny woman to deal with. Belt buckles, buttons, zippers, chains. Fuck! But hey, no underwear. That's rather hot. I claw the shit down to his ankles and unearth his mighty Excalibur.

Thunk.

This beauteous cock is everything I'd hoped for and more. A good ten inches. Nice and straight. Well-trimmed bush accents at the base of the trunk. And his balls are just the way I like 'em. Big and low hanging for optimal clit stimulation during doggie-style banging. I can't wait for these puppies to slap my lovin' nubbin silly.

I open wide and take his dick as deep as my throat will allow, which is actually pretty damn deep. I make it to within an inch of his balls, and his body loosens. "Fuck," he groans.

Who's God now? I smile inwardly. That last inch won't go to waste. I flatten my tongue, which is currently clamped like a magnet to the underside of his length, and make room. I push forward, and my lips meet the only kind of nuts I'll eat. Score!

He grabs my hair, twists, and jerks. I maintain my position, slowly moving my tongue from side to side under his shaft. He releases his breath, and tonsil fucking commences.

With each thrust, I take his cock all the way down. Swivel, suck, devour. Spit and pre-cum leak from the corners of my mouth, but I don't gag. I could do this for days. They don't call me Letty "Deep-Throat" Dillinger for nothing.

Goddamn, those balls are calling to me. Palming his dick with one hand, I face-dive into his twin jet engines, tonguing the sensitive line in between. My fingers cradle and caress his sac. Curl my tongue around and suck a hunk of nutty goodness into my mouth. Give it a little nip on its way out.

"Fuck. Me," he says.

"Gladly. But let's have another drink first."

Naked and not afraid to admit it, I head to the bathroom, snag a towel, and grab the tequila on my way back. After smoothing the towel over the plush carpet, I lie down on it and spread my legs. With two fingers, I open my pussy lips wide and pour in the tequila. He doesn't wait for an invitation.

I close my eyes and rake my fingers through his hair as he imbibes. He slurps loudly, purposefully, like he wants me to hear how much he's enjoying me. I tilt my hips to give him a better angle and force my pussy hard against his mouth. He sucks my clit, ladles tequila from my cunt with his studded tongue ...

I'm about to come again. No. Too soon.

I sit up. Fuck, I need his cock inside me.

He lunges for my mouth, pins me to the floor with his body, which I notice for the first time is rather ripped. He's not stacked like the hot gay guys I've seen outside the gym near work, but he's wiry. A scrapper. Lots of ink. I don't have the time or inclination to catalogue everything at this particular moment, but I like what I see. And feel.

His arm flails beside us. Through our sloppy drunk bites and hisses, he manages to dump out the contents of the brown bag and open the condom box one-handed. A shower of little blue packets falls next to us. I grab one, tear it open with my teeth, and spit the wrapper aside. Shades rises up, and I roll the rubber over the head of his cock.

He resumes his position on top of me, his weight divine. The tequila bottle is empty. The room spins. I'm invincible.

I grab his latex-sheathed dick and stare through his glasses as best I can. "I want you to fuck me until you're ready to come. Then you're gonna pull out and let me finish the job. You got it?"

He flashes a lopsided grin. I stroke a random tattoo. I'm so wet, I could fuck a cantaloupe and three bananas without batting an eyelash. Taking his pink soldier all the way down into my pudding trench is no biggie. But damn, it feels amazing sliding against me. I focus on that feeling, the raw sexual power darting between us. He controls the thrusts, but I control the climax.

Just how I like it.

Shades doesn't look at me as he bangs me balls-deep, which is good. I grind my hips, push my tits against him, squeeze his dick. Thank God for those Kegels I do at work when I'm bored.

Where are those toys? I feel around between grunts and kisses until my fingers hit cardboard. He drops his head to my shoulder. It's hard to concentrate with his breath tickling my ear and his beautiful cock clubbing my meat curtains like a baby seal, but I manage to rip the shit open.

Sweet fucking Jesus, Shades is a man of his word. Strap-on? Check. Dildo? Check. Lube? Check.

This motherfucker is going down.

I crack open the lube and blindly grease the silicone dick with one hand. I'm sure I'm ruining the carpet, but I don't care. Once properly oiled, I tease the dildo over my nipple. "How's it going there, buddy?"

"Aw, you know, just enjoying my daily dose of random cunt." His slow grin kills me. Pure pleasure. Pure abandon. Pure sex. Gawd.

I'm grateful I can't see his eyes. If I could, he might change my mind. I push him off and wiggle out from under him. I can't suppress the sigh that sneaks out when his cock slides free.

"Play with yourself," I tell him. "And get that condom off."

The rubber snaps and drops to the carpet. I watch him jerking off as the strap-on and I get cocked and loaded. It takes me a minute to figure out how to put the thing on. I've never worn a strap-on before, but it's ... empowering. I heft the weight of the flesh-colored love thumper, rub the flat inside behind the fake balls against my throbbing clit, and stroke it as if it's an extension of myself. Yeah, I'm digging this whole womancock thing. I shake it threateningly at him. "On your knees."

He assumes the position, ass up. Shooting a pleased, knowing grin over his shoulder at me, he somehow manages to make his impending humiliation hotter than—

Holy motherfucking shit, look at that tattoo! *Jeees*-us *Christ*-o. An inked black skeleton adorns his entire backside—neck to ankles—each line corresponding to the actual bones beneath the skin. I swallow hard. It's the most beautiful body art I've ever seen.

I'm *so* gonna fuck this guy stupid.

I squirt some more lube on this mighty cock of mine and press it against his hole before he changes his mind. Not even a flinch out of him. Gawd. Damn.

I push the head of my sili-dick past the barrier. He barely tenses. I pause and reach around to stroke him, imagining how tight he must be. For a second, I wish I had a real schlong so I could experience how it feels from the giving end of the cock.

Knowing how bad it can hurt if you're not used to the pleasure-pain of anal, I pull back to give him a quick rest and douse us both with more lube. One can never have too much when anal is involved. I enter him again, nice and slow. After a few beats, he relaxes into me. Such trust. I love this.

With an index finger, I trace the lines of both his spines. A series of notes swims through my head. I fuck him to the tune. He matches my slow rhythm.

I speed it up. Just a little.

He's still with me. Oh my God.

I fumble for his dick and pump it in time with our song.

"My balls are about to fucking explode." His gruff voice smooths into waves of erotic bliss.

"You'll come when I tell you to."

"I'll come when I damn well feel like it."

Just for that, I thrust a little harder.

His pleasure-drenched grunts get louder and faster. I

press my tits into his back, lick the scapula tattoo, and pump his ass full of me, all the while jerking him off. "You enjoy being fucked like a whore, Shades?"

He rears up, a surprise explosion of muscle and power and menace. For a second, I expect him to throw me off, but he doesn't. "We both know who's fucking who." Abrasive grit peppers the truth of his words. There's no fear or shame hiding below the surface. Shades *likes* this.

The tables turn. I suddenly feel a little used. And it's kinda hot.

Heat races to my head, addles my brain. I toss my arms around his neck and hold on for dear life like a jockey riding a bucking bronco. By God, I *will* tame this horse.

My chin rests on his back as I thrust and stroke. His jaw clenches, but the rest of his face is loose with condescension. Cock jutting, stabbing the air through my small hand, he growls—actually *growls*. The power struggle between us is both maddening and addictive.

I stretch and secure a more dominant position higher up his spine. I lick the edge of his ear, pump the head of his cock, and hump him like a horny dog. "You wanna come, don't you?"

"You want to more." His hips take over, and I no longer need to thrust. Now he's driving this train. My breath races. His muscles twist. "Do it, Lucky. Come for me. Now."

The smooth mastery in his voice forces my hand. I can't hold on any longer. This guy *owns* me, and he knows it.

Not fair. I don't want to give up first. I want him to submit to *me*—

Tough shit.

My clit succumbs to the pressure of the rubbing dildo, his slick pre-cum coating my fingers, and the seductive bass line playing in my head.

Scales tip. Reality wobbles. Tequila rules.

The orgasm rocks me from tits to stern, inside and out. Yowls burst out of my mouth like the banshee cry I utter onstage when the music really moves me.

Riding me hard, he wears a triumphant, shit-eating grin as he ushers my orgasm to conclusion. He's an evil mastermind who orchestrated the whole torrid affair, and I'm the naïve plaything who fell right into his trap.

I may have lost the battle, but I'm not going down easily.

"Your turn." My voice is like used sandpaper. Sated, but not conquered. I put some elbow grease into jerking him off and cover the head of his cock with my hand. He reaches backward, clamps his thick, straining arms around my thighs.

The bastard smiles.

Hot jizz shoots like a busted fire hydrant into the cup of my palm. I imagine filling his ass with the same and fuck him harder through his orgasm.

When the last of his ejac evacs and my knees quit shaking, I lay my cheek on his wiry shoulder.

He put on an ovation-worthy performance, but I can't have him upstage me. The final power play is mine.

I bring my hand to my mouth, open wide, and swirl my tongue through his cream, sucking down every last drop. His salty cum erupts my taste buds. I savor his flavor, commit it to memory, and swallow.

He lifts an appreciative brow. "Happy birthday, pussycat." Laughing, he collapses face down on the carpet, pants bunched around his ankles, my dick impaling him. Not a speck of modesty anywhere on the guy.

Jesus Mahalia Christ.

The swirl of tequila, cum, and dopamine grabs me by the hair, pulls me under, and drowns me. I snatch a deep, full breath and pass out on his back.

UP, DOWN, AND ALL AROUND

Buzz ... *clunk* ... *buzz* ...

Yeah, I'm buzzed.

Buzz ... *buzz* ... *clunk* ...

What the fuck is that?

Buzz ... *buzz* ... *buzz* ...

Shit. Phone?

I lift my head from a warm puddle of drool inching across a black and tanned image.

Hey, that looks like something from my high school biology textbook. Vertebrae?

Hey, there's a live body under me. Why am I ...?

I push up slowly.

Hey, I have a cock. And it's up a dude's ass.

Whoa.

I look around the fancy hotel suite. Shove red tangles out of my eyes. Wipe the cum and tequila-tinged saliva from the corner of my mouth. My head pounds with a swirl of morning-after regrets. What the fuck did I get up to last night? I mean, besides this guy's ass? And how do I free myself from this hot little medieval torture contraption strapped to my loins?

The man lying face down, impaled by my silicone love torpedo seems to be asleep, but it's hard to tell through the dark glasses he wears. His trim, muscled body displays a full-length tattoo of a human skeleton. The details and shading are fucking amazing. I slide my fingers over his scapula, and memories jolt to life.

Birthday drinks. Adult toy store. Shades.

Shades.

He makes a little sleepy sigh—the one hint of vulnerability he's relinquished since I met him—and my cooter juices like Pavlov's fucking dog. Christ, I *cannot* be here when he wakes up. Just can't.

No clue how the hell I got these straps buckled in the state I was in last night, but I did a damn fine job. So fine that I have to fiddle with the fuckers for a couple of minutes before I can shake the gear loose. Despite my efforts to leave the cock engaged, it slips out. Somehow, he sleeps through my jostling. He must've been as wasted as I was.

Gingerly crawling off his splayed form, I take a wistful look at the scene of my crimes, and my gut churns. A used but empty condom, along with eleven unopened packets pepper the carpet around him. Drained tequila bottle. A crusty towel. Torn brown bag barfing up assorted sex-toy packaging.

And *him*.

Sigh.

Hottest. Sex. Ever.

And for me to remember it that way, I have to leave. I've learned through trial and a lot of error that wanting is far more fulfilling in the long run than having, no matter how many times the "access denied" screen stabs you in the neurons when the instant replay kicks in. I look at each one-night stand as a *Veni, vidi, vici* deal. I get to keep the details of amazing sex logged in my memory banks. History gets to keep the unwanted emotional baggage those memories like to travel with.

Much as I'd love to give the walk-in shower a whirl, I'll have to bathe at home. I stand and wriggle into my jeans with lightning speed. As I reach for my shirt, a black square of leather catches my attention. His wallet. Open on the floor fifteen feet away, flashing his driver's license, which I can't see clearly from here. His life's story—condensed to a series of numbers, dates, and goddamn it, a picture of him without the shades—is within my grasp if I take six steps forward. Right there. I stare for a full minute at the white plastic card calling my name.

I turn back to Shades, sprawled on the floor. He took me places I didn't even know *existed* last night. Imagine where else we could go now that we got violating his bunghole out of the way ...

Funny thing is, despite what I did to him, he wasn't submissive in the least. He was in total control, and we both knew it.

My pussy aches for round two.

I *did* promise to return the favor on his birthday. I always keep my promises.

Maybe I should leave my number or email address...

No strings attached, Letty.

Forced apathy fills my heart and hardens the muscle into steel. Pressing my lips together, I turn away from Shades to keep from caving. I grab my shit and walk out the door, leaving behind the best dicking—physical and mental—that's ever happened to me.

The elevator ride down is uneventful. I stride to the sliding doors in the lobby and rush into the cold brightness. Thank God we returned to downtown after last night's trip to the toy store on the west side. The hotel is only a few blocks away from where I'd parked before hitting the bar.

A hot shower and breakfast, and I'll forget about the hook-up by lunch. And if that fails, there's always work tonight to throw me off Shades's track by putting me in a royally foul mood. Slinging barbeque for fat rednecks with accents so thick, they sound like they're speaking another fucking language is so inspiring. Jesus. Just thinking about work sets off my pretend angina.

I chose angina as my medical condition for calling-in-sick purposes because it sounds like vagina.

Clunk ... buzz ... buzz ...

Damn it, who's calling me at—I whip out my raggedy-ass phone and check the time. Goddamn. Eleven thirty already?

"Hello." I head down Clayton Street toward the College Avenue parking deck where I left my car. I think.

"Where the fuck have you been? I've been calling you all morning." Jillian. The band's manager, aka Hard-Ass Bitch.

"You know, up, down, all around."

"Two questions. Did you get drunk last night? And are you sober now? 'Cause I've got some *shit* to tell you."

"That sounds promising. Let me guess. Blanko cancelled our gig for next Friday." Because it would be so fucking typical of that dickhead. Can't I have just one day of non-suckery where the band is concerned? One damn day? I rub my eyes.

"Nope. *I* cancelled your gig for Friday."

I stop in the middle of the sidewalk. "What the *fuck*, Jillian?" The asshole pedestrian riding my heels runs into me. I huff and flip him off as he walks past.

Jillian pauses. "I found you something better."

"What's better than a Friday night at Vertigo Palace?"

"December, January, February, and March in every small-sized venue in the Southeast."

"Fuck. Me." I drop to the concrete. Business people in suits, college students toting coffee cups, and red-and-black-clad tourists frown and step around me, shaking their heads. "Are you telling me you booked us a ..." I don't want to say the word too loudly for fear of jinxing it, so I whisper, "tour?"

"Yep."

"Fuck me." I jump up. "Fuck me." I dance across the crosswalk, shaking my ass to a brand new celebratory bass groove in my head. "Fuck me!" More bemused stares from passersby. Fuck them too.

"Happy belated birthday." Jillian never smiles—she

claims it causes wrinkles—but I picture a teeny-tiny *Mona Lisa* grin on her face.

"Whose dick did you have to suck to get us booked?" I can't fucking believe this.

"First of all, it's not a headlining gig." Her voice takes on some reticence like a boat taking on water.

"Okay." Well, shit, no skin off my nose, I guess. We can hardly book gigs in our own hometown thanks to the influx of "creative" types—*wank, wank*—bombarding the university with amateur, here-today-gone-tomorrow bands. They proliferate like fucking viruses, lowering expectations among the beer-guzzling frat and sorority house masses. If your daddy's rich enough and knows people, he can get your band on at the bigger clubs. Meanwhile, actual *talent* gets tossed by the wayside.

"And, Kate might need convincing." Now Jillian sounds downright reluctant.

My stomach stops, drops, and rolls. Dizzy, I mount the curb, tighten my coat around me, and grab the nearest lamppost choked by unlit Christmas lights. "Why's that, Jillian?"

A long pause. "You'll be touring with Killer Dixon."

Mother fuck. Skunk fuck. God-doodle-damn it, fuck.

I close my eyes and concentrate on the cold air rushing in and out of my lungs. "Way to fatten me up only to shoot me in the ass. I'll bet you like your meat rare too. Is it too late to get back on at Vertigo Palace?"

"Now hold on a minute. It's not as bad as you think."

"So, Kate *isn't* gonna flip her fucking wig and shoot bullets from her tits when she hears this? Ain't no way I'll be in the room when you drop that bomb. Not without a bulletproof vest and tear gas to cover my escape."

Jillian sighs.

"Yeah, just what I thought." God *damn* it.

"If we frame it the right way—"

"*We?* Uh-uh. There's no *we*. There's *you*. *You* are the

manager. *You* defuse this shit bomb. That's what we pay you for."

"You haven't paid me in two months—"

"Well ..." Okay, point taken.

"—which is why you're touring with Killer Dixon. They *do* pay me. Rather well."

"You're full of shit. They *can't* be making more money than we are. They fucking suck." Okay, maybe *suck* is a harsh word, but Cherry Buzz Float is a hundred times better. And we're chicks who play gritty, raw music that actually means something. We don't need all those fancy guitar pedals, vocal digitizers, or synths. Our tunes are organic. Unfiltered. Straight from the fucking gut. We're "impure" by today's digital standards of perfection and damn proud of it. Killer Dixon? Those fuckers sound like everybody else. Nothing unique about them or their music.

"Danny OD'd one time too many, so Rax and Toombs kicked him out. The new guy has a rich daddy, marginal talent, and a huge rebellious streak. His father gave him a tour bus, a wad of cash, and his blessing. That's where we are."

I smack the back of my head against the pole. "This bites. Why'd they have to kick Danny out? Rax is the one who stole Kate's song. If he hadn't fucked us over, we'd have been headlining a year ago." I say the words, but my realism circuitry overrides the false optimism.

The truth is, the song in question wasn't all that great to begin with. But it's the principle of the thing. You don't steal someone else's shit. Period.

"As manager of *both* bands, I have a vested interest in staying neutral on this one. The song rights issue is between Kate and Rax. They've beaten this horse to death. Unless Cherry Buzz Float wants to sue, I think you should put aside your differences for the sake of the band."

"Yeah, but which band? Sounds like we're doing *them* a favor by going on tour with them."

Jillian says nothing.

I get the feeling she knows something I don't. Probably something obvious that I *should* know, but I'm too stubborn and pissed off to notice.

"Look, I know you're fond of your little … boys," I wrinkle my nose, "but Kate's not gonna budge. And neither will I." Kate might be a total psychopathic bitch, but she's my bandmate, and I have to side with her.

"Okay. If you're willing to sacrifice your dreams because of some stupid argument that happened two years ago, give 'em all up." I picture Jillian throwing her hands in the air as she always does when she gets fed up with my shit. "But I'm going with Killer Dixon, whether you do or not."

I freeze.

"That sounds a wee bit like an ultimatum." I don't do well with ultimatums. They give me really bad gas.

"It is."

My stomach gurgles.

I can't believe this. "You'd cut us loose for Killer Dixon because their new guy has *money*? This is an all-time low, even for you, Jillian. You've been our manager for four years. You're just gonna let us go?"

Shit, Jillian's the only manager we've ever had. And despite the fact that I hate her, I really like her. She kicks us in the ass when we need it and pushes us harder than we think we can go. She may be a slave driver, but if it weren't for Jillian, we would never have made it out of Kate's parents' garage.

"Like it or not, we all need Killer Dixon. They could be your ticket out of Athens. And mine too." Her voice shucks some of its edge.

My heart loses the hardness it worked up a while ago to walk out on Shades. Now it's soggy and conflicted, which just pisses me off more. I don't want to admit it, but Jillian may be right. Not about Killer Dixon being worth a shit, but about the opportunity to break out and expand our audience. We may never get another shot like this.

In order to seize the day, I may have to let go of some pride, which is a pain in the ass. It plays havoc with my mojo and shit.

I sigh. "When do you want to talk to Kate and Jinx?"

"Let's do it at rehearsal tonight."

I feel like I'm plotting a murder. Maybe I am. "Okay. I'll see you after work."

"Letty?"

"Yeah?"

"Thanks." Her voice changes with that one word. Nothing obvious like a crack, but something soft—like respect, or maybe hope—curls the edges upward.

The line clicks dead, and I stare at my ancient phone's cracked home screen. One day soon, my band's album cover will fill the blank space there. I reserved the spot when I got the cheap piece o' shite, and despite all the speed bumps, I haven't given up hoping that it's gonna happen.

It's *gotta* happen.

SHIT, MEET FAN

After an invigorating night of schlepping dry pig meat and soggy french fries for cheap-ass, dollar-tip-leaving motherfuckers, I head for the east side to Jillian's. She has a big barn behind her house where we rehearse. Nestled on three acres of farm property, Jillian's place is quiet and peaceful with no neighbors to complain about the noise. Only downside is at this time of year, you need a couple of inches of blubber to weather the cold, and my threadbare coat ain't cutting it.

Kate and Jinx started practice without me. They always do when I work late, which is fine. Saves me the trouble of listening to Kate's bitching. Wonder what it'll be tonight. I'll bet someone gave her sneaky looks in the coffee shop where she goes to write songs. Or maybe she'll go off about so-and-so dick-sucking their way onto the Vertigo Palace stage again. She's so fucking paranoid. If she weren't the best damn guitarist around, I'd have kicked her to the curb ages ago. As it is, she fucking rocks, so I tolerate her fits and mood swings.

Jillian lifts a brow at me the second I walk through the barn door. Guess it's her signal I should don my CDC-issued hazmat suit while she cranks up the industrial-sized fan.

Vroom, vroom.

Jillian lights a cigarette. She wears her usual business suit—gray slacks with sensible heels—which looks ridiculous surrounded by bales of hay and farm equipment. She's a paralegal by day but wants to get out of that biz to focus on managing her two bands. What the fuck is a paralegal, anyway? Jillian's a hard-ass broad, so I'm guessing she bitch-slaps criminals for a living. Criminals or lawyers. Same thing, really.

"Kate, I want to fill you in about the tour," Jillian says.

"Yeah, what about it?" Kate slaps her hands on her scrawny hips and knocks a wisp of black hair out of her eyes with an impatient puff. To look at her, you'd think she was a starving, coke-addict model rather than a guitarist. Well, again, same thing.

"Let's not beat around the bush. Just tell her." I back up, cross my arms, and tuck my fists loosely into my pits. If I have to start swinging, I wanna be ready.

Poor Jinx can tell shit's about to go down. Head lowered, she grabs her drumsticks and bounds off her stool.

For as hard as she beats the drums, Jinx is more timid than an abused puppy scrounging for food beside a 7-Eleven dumpster. Except when she's onstage. When she's behind her kit with the lights shining across her shoulders and sweat glistening on her skin, she's a beautiful blond blur of rage-fueled enchantment. A ninja pixie. A butcher goddess.

Not trying to be funny, but I wonder if Jinx has some kind of social anxiety problem.

Jillian pulls a heavy drag off her cigarette and exhales through her nose. The ensuing smoke cloud shrouds her face for a few seconds. She flicks the ash into an empty Diet Coke can. "You're going on with Killer Dixon, and they're headlining. Now, I know how you feel about Rax, but—"

"Oh, *helll* no." Kate backs up, cleans an invisible window with her palm, and draws a spell circle with her chin. I'm pretty sure she sucks her teeth too. "Hell. *Fuckin'.* No."

I shift weight between my feet. Jinx flat-out cowers. It's fixin' to get ugly up in here. I scan the barn for potential weapons. At least if we need to bury any bodies, there's plenty of land around.

Jillian stands from the square hay bale she's been sitting on and points with her cigarette finger. "Hear me out before you have your little hissy fit."

Suddenly, it's not so cold in the barn. Flaring tempers can do that to a place.

"I don't know what *that's* supposed to mean——" Here goes Kate's chicken-neck thing again.

"Of course, you do, Kate." Jillian's faded blue eyes pick up some extra color with the rising volume of her voice. "You're a child. When you don't get your way, you throw tantrums. You need to learn to control your anger. It would get you a hell of a lot farther in life."

Whoa. But kinda hard to argue with that point.

"And since we're on the subject," Jillian's just warming up now, "if you had let that shit with Rax go when it started two years ago, you might have obsessed a little less about everyone else flying past you up the popularity ranks and focused on how to climb to the top yourself. Face it. In this business, shit happens. I don't give a fuck about your beef with Rax. As far as I'm concerned, it's over. Move the fuck on with your life and write some goddamn music."

Kate stares slack-jawed at Jillian as if she's been slapped. Silence fills the barn as accusing gazes bounce back and forth between them.

I release the breath I've been holding and take a tentative step forward. "I'm not wild about touring with Killer Dixon, either, but it's not like we have to interact with them. We can have our side of the bus, and they'll have theirs. We go onstage. They go onstage. Pack everything up, then back to our side of the bus. No talking required."

"Rax *stole* my song, Letty." Kate's voice is cold and low and spiked with venom. "*Our* song. Possibly our

35

livelihood."

"Yeah, but what did he do with it? Did he make millions? Is he bathing in vats of champagne every night? No. That dickhead works at a fucking gas station."

The remaining words on the tip of my tongue have never been uttered. Maybe it's time they should be. I don't want to piss her off, but I can't hold it in any longer. "Did you ever stop to think maybe the song wasn't as good as we thought?"

Kate snaps her gaze to mine like a whip. The lash stings.

"Let's be honest." I glance at Jillian, whose slowing breaths back me up. "Killer Dixon is a *decent* band. Not better than us, but pretty good. They have a larger following, more songs in their catalogue, and bigger name recognition."

God, it hurts to admit this shit. My pride's been punched in the nads by the truth over and over again, but I've denied it as much as Kate. Nobody wants to hear they're not as good as they think they are. Time for us to face the facts.

"Now they've got a tour bus with space for us. Maybe it's a blessing in disguise. A new chapter in our band's history. Would it really be so bad to ride their coattails to fame and then fart in their faces when we blow past them? Hell, we could even light the farts."

Jinx lifts her head and meets my eyes from the corner of the barn. The beginnings of a smile curve the sides of her mouth. The snarl in Kate's upper lip softens a tad.

Tempers simmer down, and my sap meter rises with the flicker of a memory from when we were naïve and hopeful dreamers, before reality jaded us. "Do you guys remember our first rehearsal? The promise we swore to each other and to The Rock?"

(For those of you not in the know, The Rock is the presence in the universe that gives art its form, its power, and its immortality. Praise The Rock!)

Kate mumbles, "Light up the night with music."

"Shake the walls till they crumble to the ground," I say.

"Give the fans a reason to remember us," Jinx adds softly.

"And always leave them wanting more," Jillian finishes.

We all focus on Kate, who scowls at the dirt and smatterings of hay beneath her feet.

"What do you say, oh great bitch guitarist goddess? Will you join us in our quest to honor The Rock by putting Killer Dixon to shame onstage for the next few months?"

Kate jerks her head to the side and pops her neck. "I'd like nothing more than to knock those fucknuts down a few decibels. Especially Rax."

"Is that a yes?" Jillian puffs on her cigarette casually, like her panties never even *thought* about getting in a wad. Her bad ass probably goes commando to avoid the possibility. She's a fucking drill sergeant with an attitude problem.

"I need some time to think about it."

Jillian checks her watch. "Will five minutes do?"

The sound of car wheels crunching over gravel brings up our heads, and we all turn to the door.

"Make that thirty seconds," she says.

A bomb drops in my gut. *Please tell me you didn't invite them here, Jillian. Please.*

"I invited Killer Dixon over so we could talk about the tour." Jillian flips her cigarette into the silver can and ambles to the door. "Must be them now."

Tick-tock.

Kate's lips smash together, and she shakes her head. "Son of a bitch."

Tick-tock.

I join Kate and beckon to Jinx. Fingering her bottom lip, she slinks over. I toss my arms around my bandmates' shoulders and say, "We're better than them. We're stronger than them. And we're gonna rock harder than them. We have nothing to worry about. Let's just play nice, use the guys like the tools they are, and pluck tiny violins for their broke asses on our way to the bank. There ain't nothing they can do to put us down."

Tick-tock.

"Ladies, you know Rax and Toombs," Jillian calls. "And this is Killer Dixon's new singer-bassist, Todd Armstrong."

Tick-tock.

I look past Jinx to the three dudes darkening the doorway. The one in the middle takes off his sunglasses and hooks them on the front of his shirt beneath a black pea coat. His pouty lips settle into an amused smile when his gaze collides with mine. One pierced brow arches.

KA-BLAM!

If I had nuts, they'd have crawled so far up my ass, my breath would smell like cum.

My heart chokes on its own blood as the guy I fucked last night steps up and says, "You can call me Shades."

MAN PASTIES AND G-STRING BANANA HAMMOCKS

The motherfucker I butt-plowed last night is with Killer Dixon? No fucking way.

And he's *rich*? I guess I should've known when he took me to the fancy hotel, but I just assumed he was really horny and desperate to get his kink on. Who would've guessed a loaded dude like him would be into that sort of shit?

Kate winds her arms over her chest with a loud sigh. Fury rolls off her like heat waves over hot Georgia pavement in August.

I suppose Shades's sexual proclivities are the least of my worries at the moment.

I turn my head to the ceiling and say a silent prayer: *Sweet Baby Jeebus, if you'll have mercy on me and not let Kate find out what I did with Shades, I won't masturbate in confessional anymore, I swear. Amen.*

Jillian walks Shades—*Todd*—Rax Wrathbone, and Toombs Badcock over. The smell of leather beats the hay into submission and shits on it. The male specimens blocking our path look us over top to bottom.

"Kate, Letty, Jinx." Jillian gestures to each of us in turn.

Shades smiles and nods.

"How's it going, Kate?" Rax stuffs his hands in his jacket pockets and notches his head. He takes in her boobs with a long, unapologetic ogling.

At about six feet, he's the shortest of the three. The top layer of his chin-length black hair is pulled into a topknot. Shrewd, blue eyes. The tattooed head of a cobra poises, fangs ready to strike his neck. The rest of the serpent's body disappears under his black coat collar.

Kate told me Rax's tattoo winds around his back, down his stomach, and the tail ends at the head of his cock. I'll believe it when I see it.

Rax is the "brains" behind the Killer Dixon operation. Songwriter/thief, guitarist, sex emperor. Or so I've heard.

Kate makes a show of raking her gaze down him, a mockery of his greeting. "I'd be a hell of a lot better with a million bucks in my kitty. Thanks to you, that's not happening anytime soon."

"I missed you too. Thought this tour might be an opportunity for us to reignite our love." He licks his doubly pierced bottom lip, loudly sucks the spit off, and blows her a kiss. The two thick silver rings near the corners of his mouth look like snake fangs.

"I'm all outta love for you, big boy. The rent on you is *way* too high for a broke-ass girl like me." She thumps his dick through his jeans.

Rax grins.

Toombs's creepy silver-gray eyes shift to an empty wall as if he'd rather be testing out gasoline body lotion next to an active volcano than standing here in Jillian's barn. Like his bandmates, he's slathered in tattoos, but his ink follows a vivisection theme: a simulated slit throat with gaping stitches, burnt acid holes along his neck, peeled flaps of skin.

Pieces of barbed wire—like, from an actual fence—twine through his ears. Dried blood streaks his neck where the wire appears to have cut him.

Wow. I swallow hard.

Toombs is the scary one. The dark loner you hear stories about. They say once he finishes with a girl, she walks away changed. One touch of his cock leaves behind a shell of a woman with mental and emotional scars. Like a sexual vampire or some shit. Naturally, he's the only one of the guys in Killer Dixon I ever considered tapping like a maple tree. Well, until Shades.

I glance at him. He starts to say something. I blink three times in quick succession, and barely shake my head. If he spills what we did, Kate will walk.

His grin widens, but only around the eyes, which I can actually see now. In daylight or darkness, Todd Armstrong is the hottest piece of ass I've ever pleasured.

Wait a second.

Armstrong ... Where have I heard that name recently? It's fairly common, but ...

Shit. It can't be. It's a coincidence, surely.

I never saw him pay for the room at *Armstrong* Suites ...

Does his daddy own that hotel chain? If so, then I buggered a multimillionaire's son last night. Holy anal mishaps, Batman.

My head is dizzified. I can't even blame it on liquor tonight.

I quickly face Toombs for a distraction. He's staring at Jinx like he wants to eat her, barf her up, and save the cud for leftovers later.

Uh ... Dude makes me more than a little uncomfortable. I shake myself free of the playback running through my head and inch over to Jinx.

Jillian lays a hand on Shades's arm. "Todd, where did you say you were from?"

"Boston most recently. I grew up all over the place."

I cover my snort. I'll bet. With a rich dad, the little prince probably spent his youth jetting around the globe with a royal live-in tutor. I can't fucking believe this shit.

"Well, since you're new to Georgia, let me show you a little Southern hospitality. Let's go to the house where it's warmer. We can talk about specifics for the tour." Jillian heads to the door. Everyone follows except Shades and me.

I shake my head again and murmur, "Don't say a

word."

"Wouldn't dream of it, Lucky."

Green eyes. He has beautiful green eyes. The cooter engine revs. Pretty sure she sprung an oil leak.

Down, girl.

I zip away from him and rejoin Jinx, positioning myself between her and Toombs.

We get inside, and Jillian ushers us to the quaint, country-style living room. I make a point of sitting with Kate and Jinx on the couch.

Once everyone's seated, Jillian shakes the graying blond strands of her bob out of her face and surveys her minions. "Can I get anyone a drink? I've got beer and wine. I also made up some snacks."

"Not hungry." Rax waves her off. "I got a couple of bitches begging for a banging at home. Can we get on with this?"

Toombs cuts his gaze to Rax and leans back in his chair. A scuffed black boot crash lands on his knee.

Jillian's expression hardens. "Okay, let's not fuck around. We all know there are … tensions between you. What happened in the past is over. I have a few rules I expect to be followed. If you break them, I walk.

"You don't have to like each other. You don't have to respect each other. You don't even have to talk to each other. But when we're in public—onstage, in a restaurant, or in a goddamn alley—you will *pretend* to get along. Sing 'Kumba-fucking-ya' in your head if you have to, but outside the tour bus, you'd better smile like you all have matching best-friend necklaces."

Kate scowls. Jinx fiddles with her fingernails.

Rax's lip twitches. Toombs doesn't move an inch.

And Shades? He's grinning at me. Most likely to the tune of Joan Jett's "Do You Wanna Touch Me?" The bastard.

My twat churns out a fresh batch of batter in my

drawers.

Did he know who I was when he picked me up last night? What if he plotted our little romp from the get-go? Sneaky, devious motherfucker.

I wriggle and straighten. This whole thing stinks. My long-awaited chance to break out, and all it'll take is one slip of the lip for Shades to ruin everything. If Kate finds out about us, it's over.

Worse, what if he decides he likes me? The last thing I want is a guy hanging all over me, blackmailing me into sex with him every night.

I sneak a glance at him, relaxed into the chair like he owns the fucking world. With his dad's money, he probably owns a nice chunk of it. Smug, self-assured, cocky. Only thing he's missing is a smoking jacket, a pipe, and a bevy of Playboy Bunnies surrounding him.

But God *damn*, he's a fine piece of ass. And he certainly knows his way around the female body. Maybe fucking him every night wouldn't be *that* bad.

Shut up, Letty.

"My other rule is that while you're on tour, you'll work a forty-hour week like real people do." Jillian studies the girls on one side of the room, then the boys on the other. I feel like I'm getting chewed out by the coach in high school gym class for flushing maxi pads down the toilet. She crosses her arms over her chest. "That means during the day, you're either rehearsing or writing music."

"Oh right, so I can have my tunes ripped off by a thieving asshole again?" Kate bares her teeth at Rax. "Fuck that."

Rax sneers back.

Jillian bitch-slaps Kate with a scowl. "That's what monitor headphones are for. And there's plenty of room on the bus for you to spread out. If you want to make it, you gotta be in constant production mode. The more songs you have, the better the chance you'll get picked up when a record exec stumbles upon you. This is a *business*. You have to treat it as such. *Both* bands have been screwing around, waiting for shit to happen for too long. Shit doesn't happen. Professionals *make* it happen."

"Sounds like a challenge," Rax says, his gaze targeted right between Kate's eyes.

"I do love a challenge." Her upper lip twitches with a Billy Idol snarl.

Jillian butts in, "Good. Here's one for you: by the end of the tour, I want twelve new songs out of both bands."

"Too easy. I say we up the stakes with a friendly wager." Rax the snake coils into the couch, ready to strike. "Something that'll prove beyond a shadow of a doubt which is the better band."

Toombs shifts the side of his mouth upward in what must be his version of a grin.

Jinx's head pops up, but as usual, she doesn't say anything.

"First band to score a record deal wins a prize." Rax's hypnotic eyes almost swirl.

Kate puffs out her chest. "Writing an album is a piece of piss. But what if neither band gets a deal? I'd hate for a draw to stop me from publicly humiliating you assholes. Give me something more tangible to shoot for. Something fan-based. They're the ones we'll be playing for over the next few months. They're the ones who really matter."

"Okay. Whichever band has the most likes on their fan page by January 1 wins a prize."

"Like what?" I ask. Not that I'm worried. We'll obviously win, no beans about it. I just want to know what I'll be rubbing in Killer Dixon's faces.

Rax leans forward. "A wallow in the loser's pit of failure. A public humiliation of the viral kind."

"You mean like a YouTube video of you guys dressed in drag, giving us lap dances?" I twist a red lock around my finger and flap my lashes. I'd fucking *kill* to see Shades in a bikini and on a pole.

Rax smiles. "You're on."

"Uh—" Jinx raises her hand like the class geek. I pat her knee to hush her.

"I'm gonna love watching you in a G-string banana hammock and pasties, grinding your big cock in my face," Kate says to Rax. "I'll be sure to stock up on dollar bills. And wipe my ass on them for you ahead of time."

The grin cracks his face wide open, and he rests his arms on his knees. "Dream on, sister. We're bigger and better than you. Got way more fans already. Everyone in this room knows it's gonna be three hot bitches skidding down the pole into our waiting laps."

He turns his head thoughtfully to the window. "I think I'll write an extra-special riff for you to solo-strip by, Kate. Or maybe I'll use the one from the song you tried to steal from me."

Kate bounds out of her seat, shoots across the room, and stops in front of Rax. Her hands ball, weight shifts, and shoulders heave. He lurches up, furious fire burning his eyes, and plants his nose an inch from her face.

Oh shit.

I stand. Shades stands.

"You stole that song from *me*." Kate's lips miss Rax's by a hair.

"Bullshit. You were so stoned that night, you could barely hold your head up, let alone write a fucking song."

"Chill out, guys." Jillian darts over to referee. She burrows in and pushes the two of them apart. "Cut this shit out *now*. Both of you."

Kate huffs. "Make me."

"Okay, get out." Jillian points at the door. "Get the hell out of my house, and don't come back until you can pretend to be an adult."

"Fuck you. I don't need you or your fucking tour.

Shove it up your ass." Red-faced, Kate grabs her coat, flips off the room on her way out, and slams the door hard enough to rattle the jamb behind her.

Great.

There's no way Kate's getting on that bus now. Biting my tongue, I scowl at Rax.

Jillian takes a deep breath, sits, and lights another cigarette. She combs her fingers through her hair. "Kate will come back once she has time to think about it. She always does."

I'm not so sure. She's pretty pissed.

Rax shrugs and rubs his hands together like nothing ever happened. "Well, our work here is done. Gotta be off. We have a headlining tour to get ready for."

Toombs stands and stretches. Shades follows. The smug dickweeds.

"Nice to meet you, ladies," Shades says. His smartass tone and total disregard for our situation crawl under my skin. *He's* blowing *me* off? What the fuck?

Toombs licks his lips and surveys Jinx like a slab of meat in a butcher's window. "Jinx."

A blush slides down her face, and she looks away fast, gnawing on her already cut-to-the-quick fingernails.

The trio of male bodies with egos big enough to fill a museum marches out, all smiles and attitude.

I can't think of a single insult to hurl at them. I must be in shock. I turn to Jillian. "What the hell just happened here?"

She looks after the guys and shakes her head. "Don't worry about it. Stick to the original plan. It'll work out."

"I'm not touring without Kate."

Jinx pipes up, "Me neither." I'm glad she's with me on this.

"I know she's a bitch and hard to get along with, but we can't replace her." I resume my seat. Dread sinks into my gut, weighing it down. Maybe it wasn't meant to be.

I stare blankly at the wall. Another dream shattered, just when the Technicolor was about to kick in.

I'm going to be a fucking waitress for the rest of my life.

Gulp.

My brain doesn't know what to settle on. Yesterday, I sat in a bar bemoaning my lack of music success, blowing my birthday wish on fantasies of making it big. I forgot my troubles when I shoved my fake dick up Shades's ass. Then this morning, I find out I'm going on tour. But it's with a bunch of dickheads I hate. Except maybe one of them. And now the tour's off, so none of it matters.

Right back where I started.

I want off this roller coaster. I need to think. Or not think. Something.

"I'm out of here." I pick up my coat and sling it around my shoulders. Memories of Shades warming me with his ugly-ass pea coat in the taxi last night smack the back of my head. I shiver.

Jillian rubs her forehead. "What about rehearsal?"

I point to Kate's empty spot on the couch. "Kinda hard to practice without a guitarist. What's the point, anyway?"

A staring contest ensues. I win.

"Bye, Letty," Jinx says softly.

My heart breaks a little for her, but I head for the door anyway. "Bye, Jinx."

Outside, my foggy breath puffs around me. I wish I'd nabbed a few of Jillian's beers before I walked out. Might make the carnage of the last twenty-four hours a little less vivid.

On my way to the POS I've been driving since I got my license nine years ago, I pause and look up at the stars. They're so bright out here, away from the city lights. So different without the blight of civilization to diminish their glory.

Sometimes I think Kate diminishes Jinx and me. She dictates what happens with this band because she knows we can't go on without her. And if, God forbid, we disagree—about anything—then we're "against her."

Fuck that.

I get in the car, twist the key in the ignition, and wait for the old girl to sputter to life. It takes three tries before the bitch finally turns over.

My ass is freezing. The heater doesn't work. I rub my hands together and step on the gas pedal to rev the engine a few times.

My heart hurts.

I don't want to go home. It's too depressing to drink alone.

So, back to the bar I go. Along the way, I vow not to pick up any guys tonight and to have only one drink. Something really cheap.

I snag a parking spot on Clayton Street right outside BAR-k and rush into the warm, dark cave where drunken losers go to drown their sorrows. I should invest in this place for all the time I spend here. Maybe some day, when I'm rich and famous.

I plop my ass down on a stool in front of Rob.

"Hey, Letty. How's it going? You have fun last night?"

"Not really," I lie. "Gimme the cheapest beer you got."

Rob nods, pulls down a glass, taps the keg, and hands me a mug of frosty goodness. "That guy you left with. He came in here today."

I choke midslurp. The violent twitch of my beer-holding hand sloshes a thick, foamy mustache onto my upper lip. I slog it off with my sleeve and shake the bubbles to the floor beside me. "What? When?"

"Couple hours ago."

"Was he looking for me?"

He shrugs. "He didn't mention you."

Shit, why do I care?

I don't. I suck down a big gulp.

Motherfucker didn't ask about me. *Pfft.* Just for that, I oughta write a song about him.

I set down the beer and bust out a rhythm on the wooden bar top with palm slaps. Wiggling my ass on the stool, I put my back and hips into it. The neck joins in the rocking. Words surf along on my brain waves. I mumble bits and pieces.

> *I take you down, kick off your crown*
> *My boot crushes your chest, you lie there and wallow*
> *You can hide those eyes, your precious prize*
> *But anywhere I go, you're sure to follow*
> *Tonight, it's you and me in our own little world*
> *Just 'cause it's casual don't mean it's hollow*
> *When I do my worst, you're gonna burst*
> *Deal with your guilt when I'm gone tomorrow*

The two guys sitting at the bar look at me as if I've grown three heads. Then one of them—the white-haired dude who looks about seventy—starts rocking to the beat too. "Get it, girl!" he yells.

I up the volume on my lyrics.

> *Aim this rocket, no time to cock it*
> *Got you in my sights, now it's time to rock it*
> *I ain't got all night, don't put up a fight*
> *Come over here and plug your prong into my socket*

Oh ho! Brilliant!

"Rob, you got a pen and paper I can use?"

He lifts a brow and tosses a few cocktail napkins in front of me. Then he shuffles around under the bar and produces a dull pencil. It'll do.

I scribble the words as fast as I can, spanking a knee with my free hand to keep the bass rhythm in my head going. In a mad fury, I jot down the musical notes too. I have to skip some to keep up with the song that shows no signs of slowing down.

I wonder what *Todd* will think of this when he—

Nope. Not going there. If, by some miracle, we do end up touring together, this song stays under wraps until it's finished and polished. Kate might be a paranoid freak, but after the two-year drama with Rax, I'm a little paranoid too. Can't risk those dickholes stealing another tune. And this bass line is fucking perfecto. Jinx will come up with a totally badass rhythm. I'll bet we can persuade Kate with it.

Yeah, this song is gonna fucking rock.

As my brain spurts out the last of its musical splooge on the napkin, the old coot at the end of the bar gets up and dances. He holds his beer high and shakes his ass, albeit slowly. Dude *might* have, like, six teeth in his head.

"Yeah, baby, you know what I'm talking about." I lift my glass in his honor and down a few more swallows. I swagger over to the guy and dance with him. I'm probably the most action he's seen in twenty years.

Rob turns up volume on the '70s radio station, drowning out conversations and bringing curious stares from customers. Zeppelin's "The Crunge" rattles the speakers. You can't dance to that song for shit, but I do anyway. And the old fucker is right here with me, swinging his bony hips, waving his scrawny arms. Man, this is what rock 'n' roll is all about.

Pretty soon, everyone in the place is head bopping or flat-out grooving. I jump on the bar, use my thumb as a mic, and belt out the song with my buddy Robert Plant.

People say Cherry Buzz Float is like a female version of Led Zeppelin. I take that as a high compliment. When they say my voice is a cross between Plant's and Janis Joplin's, I hump legs.

All eyes turn to me as I spout lyrics, grind my hips, and

put my rock moves to good use. It might not be a big arena or even the little stage at Vertigo Palace, but in this moment, I'm the fucking Queen of the World.

When the song ends, claps, cheers, and whistles warm the room. A bead of sweat rolls down my cheek. "Thank you guys for coming out. You've been great," I joke, and then bow.

Smiling, I jump to the floor. I might be glowing. I'm not sure. Definitely got a contact energy high from the small crowd. Boozers and frat boys return to their seats. The volume drops to normal. I turn around, and there's fucking Shades standing next to my seat.

HAND JOB? BLOW JOB? RIM JOB?

"Not bad for a girl," Shades says. No sunglasses, so I get the full effect of his hotness. If he weren't such a dick, it might blind me.

"I could say the same about you after what I did to you last night." I snarf down the remainder of my beer and flash my last ten-dollar bill at Rob. So much for eating this week. "I gotta cash out."

Rob waves me off and nods to the window where people on the sidewalk peer inside through cupped palms. A few wander in. "After that performance, it's on the house."

Thank God. Tomorrow I feast on ramen noodles. "Thanks, bud. I appreciate that." I slap his outstretched hand, point at him, and hike up my hood over my hair. Pushing past Shades, I make my way around the tables to the door and half hope he follows.

I step into the cold night and head to the car.

Oh shit. My song. I left it on the bar.

"Fuck!"

Heart pounding like a bass drum, I turn around and run slap into Shades.

He looks down his nose and grins. "Forget something?" The napkin with my badass tune is nestled between his index and bird fingers. He wiggles them.

I grasp for the makeshift paper. He snatches it out of reach.

I sigh. "What do you want? Hand job? Blow job?" I don't say rim job, but it's not entirely out of the question. Especially considering he could be holding my livelihood in his hand.

"Food."

That's the worst idea ever. Now that the paranoia bug has bitten me, I scan the street for Kate. If she sees us together, she'll go ballistic. "Is that a code word for 'sex'?"

"No. It's a code word for, 'I'm hungry.'"

"I don't mix business with pleasure. Look, man, in case you haven't guessed, it's been a rough night. I just want to go home and crash. Alone. Can I please have that back?"

"After dinner." He walks toward the burger joint around the corner on College Avenue. Okay, I'll admit it. I check out his ass. No shame in that. It's not like I haven't seen it—or done it—before.

I catch up and fall in step with him. He doesn't acknowledge me. This guy is so weird. I can't tell if he wants me or wants to kill me. Either way, I've got two perfectly good reasons to avoid him. But after my brush with popularity in the bar, I *need* that napkin more than I'd like to admit.

"Why didn't you tell me you owned the hotel?"

"I don't own any hotels." He looks straight ahead.

"Okay, then your *dad* owns the hotel."

"How exactly is that information relevant to two strangers meeting up for a shag?"

"Most guys would brag about being rich."

He turns his head enough for me to see both of his eyes, but they focus on something past me. "I'm not most guys."

I raise a brow. "Clearly."

The gentleman holds open the glass door to the '50s-themed restaurant. Wearing a tight white T-shirt with a short black miniskirt in the dead of winter, the cute hostess with all manner of piercings and tattoos escorts us to a black pleather booth. She sizes up Shades, hands us two oversized menus, and sashays toward her perch behind the register near the door. His gaze latches onto her ass and burrows in with heat so strong, I can feel it across the table.

She tosses a glance over her shoulder to him. The harpy.

Where did that come from? Gotta be PMS.

Focus, Letty.

"So, Daddy's poor little rich boy is buying me dinner, then giving back the napkin he stole. Right?" I pray he hasn't read the lyrics on said napkin.

He rests his elbows on the table and leans forward a tad. "Let's be clear. Last night was a bash-and-dash. I heard you say it was your birthday. You were alone. I was horny, and I felt kind of sorry for you, so I banged you."

I drop my jaw and crank my neck. "*Excuse me?*" Motherfucker did *not* just insinuate that I was a sympathy fuck. Not after the reaming I gave his ass. And bash-and-dash? *I* was the one who left *him* this morning.

"You said 'no strings attached.'" He targets me with his unnerving green stare.

I meet his bid and raise it. "And I meant it."

"I'm glad we agree. There's enough friction between our bands already. No need to cause anything else to fester."

A new kind of heat flames up my neck and straight out my mouth. "The only thing that's gonna fester is your ass when you get taken to the hospital for emergency boot removal surgery. But you'd probably like that, wouldn't you?"

"I might dig it, yeah." He grins.

"Yo, hep cat, 1970 called, and they want their jive talk back. What are you? A Jimi Hendrix throwback?" I cross myself and make prayer hands. "Not that there's anything wrong with the Great God Jimi, mind you," I lift my face respectfully to the heavens while choirs of angels sing in my head, "but those words coming from your rich white boy mouth make you sound like a total jelly roll."

He shrugs. "I like to get down with the jelly roll. But you already know that, don't you, pussycat?" A gleam sparkles in his eye.

Okay. I know how to play this game. I settle into the booth and fold my arms over my chest. "I wonder what Rax and Toombs would think about what I did to you with that strap-on. Two rough-and-tumble dudes like them with a new guy to break in? I doubt Killer Dixon's *fans* would be happy to learn their new sex god singer is a bottom for chicks with rubber dicks. That would *not* look good on your resume, buddy." I snag a piece of ice from my water glass and crunch it loudly.

The intensity in his gaze sharpens to a laser point. The burn is tangible. "What makes you think they don't already know?"

Shit. Course change. "Was sex with me a dysfunctional-rich-person thing? A Band-Aid for your negative father complex? Here's my take on it. You tried to top me from bottom because you have to be in control—a byproduct of years of privileged living, no doubt—but you also wanted a walk on the wild side, so you agreed to take a bumming as some sort of rebellion against your daddy."

"Ah, Letty. I'm a piece of glass to you. Guilty as charged." He smirks and looks away.

"Are you ready to order?" A bored-looking waitress taps her pen on a pad of paper.

"Yeah. You got any Boston butt?" I nail Shades with a glare. "I *love* to tear up some Boston butt. Maybe with a side of shredded cheese. Mmm, mmm good."

"We sell burgers here."

"Fine. Gimme one of those with some fries. And a chocolate malt." Since he's paying, I may as well go wild.

Wait, he's paying, right?

Shit. I have exactly ten bucks to my name. I start plotting my getaway.

"I'll have the same." Shades passes the menus to the chick, and she wanders off.

I study Shades's bored expression. Well, this is going great. Since this may be my last chance to put it all out there, I cut loose another barrage of burning questions. I'll probably never see him again. Nothing to lose. "Tell me something. Did you know who I was when you picked me up last night? Was it some kind of head game for you? The truth."

He meets my direct stare. "I had no idea."

"Hell of a coincidence, don't you think?"

"Yep."

"You don't sound surprised."

"I'm not."

"Because—?"

"Because you're not Lucky. I am. Things *always* go my way, even when they don't."

"I don't follow."

He drapes an arm across the back of the booth. "You don't follow good luck? It's a pretty simple concept."

"Perhaps an example is in order? I *am* just a girl, after all."

"I've been playing bass since I was a kid. I wanted to be in a band—mostly because I knew it would chap my dad's ass if I didn't follow in his footsteps. Teenage rebellion thing. Whatever. But as I learned more and more, things changed. Turned out I actually *enjoyed* music. Creating, playing—the whole scene. Totally pissed my parents off, but at that point, I was like, 'Fuck 'em.' I'm decent at something that doesn't involve hostile takeovers or wearing a suit. I'll take it.

"Before I knew it, I got good on bass. I discovered I could carry a tune. I thought, 'Shit, maybe I can make an honest career out of this.' So, I kept at it. Joined a few bands. Got some experience.

"I hooked up with a couple of cats when I moved

here, but I wasn't feeling their vibe. I told them I wanted out after this last gig, and they were cool with it.

"We open for Killer Dixon. After the show, I talk to Rax. Just casual shit. Nothing music-related. But once he warms up to me, he says he and Toombs are thinking about booting their singer. He likes my style and my voice. Maybe we can get together and jam sometime. Cool. Whatever. I figure he's full of shit.

"A few days later, I get a phone call. Killer Dixon is auditioning musicians. So, I go and play. They like what I got and offer me the front man position on the spot. We rehearse. I learn their songs. We write a few more. Things gel. And here I am.

"See? Lucky." He opens his hands like the world is his fucking oyster. Must be nice to have it so good.

I frown. "It takes more than luck to make it in this business. I guess if you have plenty of cash, you're set. Musicians like me have to work our asses off to get anywhere, and when we do break through to the next level, there's a whole new tower of shit waiting to greet us. Nothing's easy for us little people." God, he makes me feel small. I hate that feeling.

He scowls, and the pitch of his voice rises. "That's exactly why I'm doing this. I want to prove to my dad and all the doubters that I'm more than a snotty rich kid with no talent. I'm here to show him I don't need his money to make it. Whatever it takes to win, I'll do it, but I won't grease any palms. I'm playing fair because it's the only way to earn my old man's respect."

Wank, wank, wank. Mr. Moneybags has officially crawled under my skin. He's not in it for the music. He's in it for the pussy. All male musicians are. "Your dad gave you a fucking tour bus. How is that playing fair?"

"It was his parting gift. I couldn't say no. That would be insulting."

I shake my head. What a hypocrite. "I rest my case."

58

Yep, Shades is exactly like every other spoiled rotten Richie Rich I've ever met. What a disappointment.

He shifts in his seat, and apathy neutralizes his expression. "I'll be straight with you. I don't care if Cherry Buzz Float comes along for the ride or not. In fact, I'd be a lot better off if you didn't. But, if you do, we'll show no mercy. If I have to mop the stage with your sweat at every gig to win more fans, I'll fucking do it. I'm here to win, and I'll walk all over you, your friends, and anyone else who gets in my way. So, no offense if I kick your ass and thoroughly humiliate you onstage every night. It's nothing personal."

"I think you overestimate yourself." *You smug prick.*

"I don't. Jillian says we've got a record deal in the bag. It's just a matter of finding the right label."

I laugh. "Jillian said that because you're loaded. She'll kiss your ass from here to Kingdom Come as long as you keep shitting green her way."

"She said that before she knew I had money."

What? No fucking way. "Wait a minute. Jillian didn't know who you were when you joined Killer Dixon?"

He shrugs. "When she heard our new tunes, she said it was a shame we couldn't go on the road because we'd make a fortune. That was when I told her I had a bus."

Shit. Then Killer Dixon might be worth a shit after all. Jillian must *really* believe in them. She doesn't give compliments. Ever.

So, inviting us on tour wasn't a dollar sign-driven ploy to help Cherry Buzz Float. It was the opposite. Jillian felt sorry for us and used her pull with Killer Dixon's newfound cash cow to drag us along behind.

Jealousy tangoes with my hope circuitry and shorts it out. In this moment I hate Shades and his stupid fucking band. I hate them because they're better than we are. And I'm supremely pissed at Jillian for taking pity on us. We don't need pity. We need *belief*. Belief that we know how to rock with the best of them. Belief that we're not the talentless hacks I suddenly fear we are.

I scoot out of the seat. "I gotta go. I've lost my appetite. Thanks for …" I look at the empty table, my empty hands, and my empty fucking life. "Nothing."

He holds up the napkin as I race past.

Squeezing my lids shut to keep the tears from falling, I toss over my shoulder, "Keep it. I don't need it."

INTERLEWD ONE

Radio silence on the Cherry Buzz Float front continues for several days. I assume the worst because I'm too chickenshit to call Jillian. I know what she'll say anyway, and frankly, I don't want to face the truth.

I'm fucking devastated. Another gigantic stop sign in the endless, pointless cycle of my career. People wonder why musicians and artists turn to drugs and alcohol. Why they blow their fucking heads off or drown in their own puke. *This* is why. If bad reviews, snubs from record companies, and lukewarm receptions from fans don't kill you, mutiny will.

I put so many years into this band, and one deadly blowup from Kate vaporized everything I worked for. I feel like I've lost a limb.

After spending the week curled in the fetal position, drowning in a well of self-pity, I sprout a pair of pea-sized womanballs and steal a day-old newspaper from work. I figure it's time to get serious about my life since the music segment of this comedy show has been cut due to lack of funding. Plus, the lease agreement on my shitty apartment in Crack Alley ends in a couple months. It would be great to make enough money to upgrade to Dream-On Heights where the roaches are smaller and the junkies only come out at night instead of sitting on other people's stoops all day long.

Morning coffee in hand and tattered slippers on my feet, I plop down on my moth-eaten sofa and turn eagerly to the classifieds section. Let's see … credit union assistant manager. Truck driver. Hospital pharmacist.

Communications technician. Accounting supervisor.

I shuffle the pages. Where are the jobs for uneducated lowlifes? Athens is a fucking college town. Surely, there's *something* available for high school grads. There has to be.

I scan farther down the page. More of the same. On and on it goes. There aren't even any decent waitressing jobs for higher-end restaurants.

I toss the paper aside. I am so fucked.

My cell flops weakly across the table like a fish out of water. The thing produces more of a sporadic cough than a vibration, and I can't afford another one. Hell, my mom took over monthly payments on this one until New Year's. It was her Christmas present to me last year. No idea what I'll do when January 1 rolls around. The way things are going, I'll have to either live without a blasted phone or not eat.

I snatch up the infernal device. "Hello?" I growl into the speaker.

"Hey, Letty. It's Jinx." She's quieter than usual.

My anger quells, and I sigh. "Hey, girl. How's it going?"

"It kinda sucks."

"Yeah. Same here."

"You talk to Kate or Jillian?"

"Nope."

"Me neither."

"Why'd you call, Jinx? I gotta leave for work pretty soon."

"I—I don't really know why. I guess I just missed you." Her voice trembles.

My vision blurs unexpectedly, and I choke up. I plug my nose between finger and thumb to stop the sudden tingling there. Doesn't work. Stupid tear ducts decide to go into unauthorized mass production. The bastards. "I miss you too."

"Is it really over? I mean, are we … broken up?"

I wipe the drops away with my sleeve. "I don't know what we are, but I think it's safe to assume we're broken up until we hear otherwise."

"Okay." Jinx says the word so softly, I almost don't hear it. A long pause follows. "I guess I'll talk to you later. Bye." The line dies.

I pull the phone back at stare at it for a solid minute.

Who really got screwed in all of this band drama? Jinx. I've known her forever, and I understand how her mind works. She holds shit in and takes it out on her drums. Now she can't even do that because the goddamn drums are what brought her down in the first place. She must be devastated. An innocent kicked to the curb by her insensitive pimp Jillian.

Fuck Jillian. Fuck Kate. And fuck that asshole Shades for making me doubt myself.

Now I'm pissed. I guess it's better to be pissed than a quivering blob of delicate emotion in desperate need of a maxi pad.

I stomp to my tiny bedroom, dig through the dirty clothes pile for a work uniform. Naturally, I haven't been to the Laundromat this week because—*gasp!*—I ran out of quarters. I drag out my least stained Fat Johnny's T-shirt and a pair of khaki pants and put them on. No underwear. Who needs the shit? With a quick stop in front of the mirror, I twist my hair and tie it into a ponytail on top of my head. Red swishes across my shoulders as I shake the topknot hard. I throw on makeup, brush my teeth, and swig some mouthwash.

Coat, purse, keys. Off to work I go, thinking about Jinx the whole way.

I hate feeling helpless. But what else can I do? Yes, I could call Jillian or Kate and try to smooth things over, but I'm sick of playing the negotiator. People in my life need to start pulling their own fucking weight. I can't be everything to everyone. I have to look out for myself.

Still, I can't help wondering whether Jinx is okay. She's always been quiet, but today is different. What if she's depressed? Suicidal? Shit, what if her call was a cry for help, and I blew her off?

I feel like I'm at a crossroads—for both my personal and professional lives. Two choices flash before my eyes in gaudy neon: Stay where it's safe and comfortable but uninspired, or go and risk everything to make my dreams come true, even though the odds are stacked against me.

Rob's advice on the night of my birthday pops up like a footnote: *If you can't beat 'em, join 'em.*

That shit goes against my core principles, but some rules were made to be broken.

For the good of The Rock.

At a stoplight, I grab my phone and dial Jillian. She answers after two rings.

"Is it too late for us to change our minds about the tour?" My heart pounds, and I'm breathless. I might be having a mini panic attack.

"Yes. No. I don't know." Frustration laces Jillian's voice. "Where are you?"

"On my way to work. Can you set up a meeting with Jinx and Kate tomorrow night?"

"I can try."

"Call Jinx first. Tell her it was your idea. I think she's pretty down. It would help if you told her you support us, even if you don't."

"What the hell kind of shit is that?" Jillian assumes her mama-bear tone. "You think I don't support you?"

I think you feel sorry for us, I want to say, but I don't. "I think you're brown-nosing Killer Dixon because they have money." Let Jillian infer whatever she wants from that comment. It's better than telling her I know the truth. "But it's okay. I get it. You can't make money without spending money, and Cherry Buzz Float has none. So, I forgive you for being a bitch to us and taking their side."

"I do *not* take sides. You know how I feel about you."

I snort. "I do?"

"If you expect me to coddle you and hold your hand during every single rainstorm, you hired the wrong manager. You want to know the real reason I went out of my way to organize this tour for you?"

"Yeah, I do." This ought to be good.

"I did it because I believe in your music and your message, despite the cat fights, the paranoia, and bitchiness. How many all-girl rock band trios are out there today? I can't think of a single one that's had more than marginal success.

"Letty, your voice ... it's like estrogen-steeped gravel. So rough and raw, yet so feminine. And it actually sounds melodious when you sing. You've got a fucking gift. And Jinx ... I don't have to tell you how amazing she is. She's better than ninety percent of the guy drummers I've heard, and she's by far the best female. *Nobody* tops her. Kate's equally talented on guitar, and her ability to write quality music with perfect hooks is unmatched."

Wow. Just wow. I'm speechless for a few seconds.

"I had no idea you felt this way about our music, Jillian."

"Then you should pay closer attention."

"You're not exactly forthcoming with the praise."

"When I'm not criticizing you, consider it praise."

I laugh. I really do love to hate this bitch.

"The truth is—and so help me Christ, if you ever repeat these words, I'll deny them until I'm on my deathbed—I view Killer Dixon as the means to Cherry Buzz Float's end. They're good. You're better. But they have testicles and money. You don't. A supporting tour is the best I can do for you in this situation. When you start selling out shows and making money for yourselves, we'll talk about headlining. Until then, this is the way it's gotta be. If you refuse, I'll understand.

"But before you make any decisions, I want you to remember something. You're not the only one making sacrifices here. I quit my decent-paying job with benefits to manage this tour, these bands. I'm in it for the long haul. Are you?"

I feel like I've been climbing a mountain with anvils chained to my back. I'm nowhere near the top, but I can see the peak up there with the sun shining behind it. Taunting me. Daring me to defy it. With a rush of adrenaline and determination, I give it all I've got, throw off those motherfucking shackles, and smile as they fall.

Good riddance.

Opening for Killer Dixon may not be the optimal solution to our problems, but it'll give us an advantage we didn't have before.

"Yes. I'm all in. Balls to the wall. I'm pretty sure Jinx is too. You get Kate on board, and I swear I'll channel every bit of The Rock I have inside me. Every show. Every night. Every town. I want to *make* it, Jillian."

I feel her smile through the pause. "That's what I thought. Rehearsal tomorrow night. Tour bus leaves Friday morning. Your first gig is that night in Columbia, South Carolina.

"Pack your bags, Letty. Your real life is about to begin." Jillian snickers and hangs up.

Fuck, yeah.

NEED A HAND?

I have no idea what line of bullshit Jillian used to sway Kate, but Queen Bitch agreed to come on tour.

Tensions were at DEFCON 4 during rehearsals the last few days and rose steadily as the week wore on. Today as we wait in Jillian's dirt driveway, surrounded by big-ass drum cases, freezing our tits off, we're on a collision course with DEFCON 3.

Killer Dixon is late.

Kate's not the only one who's pissed. Every time Jillian blinks, the friction from her lids scraping her corneas produces sparks. I stand way clear while mentally snickering.

My thoughts haven't given Shades the pleasure of my company since we parted ways a week ago. He made it pretty clear I was nothing more than a fuck doll to him, which makes us even-Steven. Besides, I don't need the distraction of his hotness to prevent me from reaching my goals. The next few months are all about The Rock. *Long live The Rock!*

Jillian flicks the ash off the end of her cigarette and squashes the glowing red cherry into the gravel with the toe of her sensible black Oxford. She glances at her watch for the umpteenth time. "Ten thirty."

Not just late. Thirty minutes late. I smile inwardly because an outward smile would indicate I'm pleased, and I don't want to suggest I have anything but angelic intentions toward our motherfucking touring buddies. But damn, I hope Jillian gives it to them. She runs a tight ship, and tardiness is her number-two pet peeve, after incompetence.

Jaw rippling, Kate looks like she's about to bite clean through her tongue.

Jinx sits on her bass drum case, drawing pictures with the heel of her boot in the dried red clay. I smile at her. She smiles back, then looks away.

A loud engine rips open the silence like a chainsaw, and a big, honkin' bus barrels down the drive. It's ugly as sin with huge, tacky blue flames painted down both sides burning up Killer Dixon's poor attempt at a hard rock band logo.

Wow. Just wow.

The hunk of metallic penis envy rolls to a halt. The door opens, and the members of Killer Dixon swagger out.

"You're late." Jillian gathers her bags and shoves them into Rax's open hands.

"We had to stop for—"

"No excuses. I don't want it to happen again. Are we clear?"

"Yes, Mother." Rax rolls his eyes and makes a blow job motion when she turns away.

Shades is dressed in faded jeans, a black leather jacket, and of course, the sunglasses. There's a haughty air about him today. He oozes confidence. He's on the prowl. Maybe knowing this tour wouldn't be happening if it weren't for him gives him an extra shot of confidence. And something to hold over my head.

I thought for sure I was done with him, but he's still tripping my goddamn trigger. Even harder than before.

Fuck.

I give him a quick nod, pretending to be cool while my sex drive approaches a meltdown. He totally ignores me. I feel like a dickhead cricket rubbing my legs together, chirping for a mate who ain't interested.

Yeah? Well, fuck that. I'm not interested, either. Nope.

Nada. Forget it.

He leans against the bus. His tall frame taunts me. The cute messy hair, the piercings, the tattoos call to me. His ambivalent attitude grabs me by the tits and squeezes.

Motherfucker.

A rotund bald guy climbs down the steps and shakes Jillian's hand. "I'm the driver, Freddie. Nice to meet you."

"Jillian Frost. That's Letty Dillinger, Kate Pickens, and Jinx Hardwick." She gestures at us in turn. "Are you ready to go?"

Freddie nods. "Yep. I'll help you get your gear loaded."

He walks around back to a trailer humping the bus's ass and opens it. We move the cargo—with no help from Killer Dixon—and then head for the door. I'm anxious for a distraction from Shades's hotness. Let's see what the setup is like inside.

Shades hops up the steps first. When everyone's on board, he turns to us. "Guys are on the left. Dolls are on the right."

My eyeballs bulge at the scene before me. Directly behind the driver's seat is a communal area with two floor-mounted tables on either side and black leather couches hugging the walls. There's seating for four at each table, and the couches are big enough for sleeping or fucking on.

Next is the kitchen. It's small, but it utilizes space well. Cupboards above, refrigerator/freezer below. Microwave and hot pot on the counter separating them. A little pantry to the left.

Behind the kitchen are bunks with trundles for storage. Stacked two high, with four to a side, each has a black privacy curtain. Not much room for bedmates. Oh well, my prospects are shit right now anyway. I peek at Shades again. Still hasn't so much as faced my general direction since he and his buddies arrived. Jerk.

I wander to the ass end of the bus. More seating—perfect rehearsal space—buffers the sleeping area. The very back is topped off with a claustrophobic nightmare of a shower with a clear glass door on the left side. Nice. These perverts think they're gonna get an eyeful of Letty Dillinger test-driving the detachable showerhead on her cooch? Fuck them. Creative placement of a few Hendrix posters will take care of that. At least the toilet is sectioned off on the right. Sink in the middle.

As Kate and Jinx continue checking out the marvels of Shades's going-away present from Daddy Dearest, I push past and head for the bunks. "Which one is yours?" I ask Toombs.

He points to the last one on the bottom left. I toss my backpack and guitar case onto the opposite bed on the right and get up close and personal with him. He smells like cinnamon gum.

"Jinx is off limits," I say softly while everyone else is busy drooling. "Why don't you try Kate instead?"

His gaze flickers to my pixie friend and nearly burns a hole through her. Something menacing flashes behind his silvery devil eyes. His nostrils twitch. "Gentlemen prefer blondes."

"Well, when you find a gentleman, be sure to introduce him."

Kate wriggles between us with a grunt. She climbs into the bed above mine and snaps the curtain shut. Naturally, *I* get the bitch for a bunkmate. But at least this sleeping arrangement will keep Toombs away from Jinx. I don't trust him, and I definitely don't like the way he ogles her.

"If you guys are ready, I'm gonna get rolling," Freddie calls from the front.

"Rock on," Rax says.

The engine cranks up. Jinx claims the bottom bunk adjacent to mine, and Jillian stuffs her purse in the space above Jinx.

"Since we've got several hours of driving, it might be a good idea to get in a little rehearsal time," Jillian says. "I'm still not happy with the bridge on 'Take It Like a Man.'"

Kate's curtain slides open. "Where do you propose we do that?"

Jillian gestures to the tables. "Hop to it." She claps her hands twice.

Kate frowns and slides down from her perch. She puts a cap on her attitude and moseys to the front. Jinx follows. I'm not sure what the guys are doing in the back, and I don't care.

No, really. I don't. I'm here to rock with my girls.

Kate settles down on the couch and plugs into her monitor. She puts on headphones. Jinx whips out her electronic tabletop drum kit and joins her.

I wonder how Jillian convinced Kate to join us on the tour. Kate's not her usual stabby self. If she had a tail, its tip would be in her mouth. Interesting.

I crack open my bass case and join the chicks for an epic practice/jam session. When my growling stomach prompts me to check my watch, I nearly shit myself. One thirty? Where the hell did the day go? Guess I got caught up in The Rock. That's a great thing.

I look out the front window. Freddie pulls into the lot at the venue, parks, and shuts down the engine. Chills race up my arms. Holy shit. This is it. We're playing a gig someplace outside of Athens, Georgia. People don't know us here. But they will after tonight.

I smile. Hell, yes.

The guys announce they're going for burgers down the street. The girls ask if I want to grab food, but I can't fucking afford it. I politely decline and retire to my bunk for some rest.

When everyone's gone, I grab one of the cheap protein bars I packed and eat it too fast. Still hungry, I look around for a distraction. I can't devour my entire food stash on the first day of the tour.

Music. That ought to send my mind in a different direction.

I shove in my earbuds, pull up my '70s playlist, and crank up the ancient iPod. A few minutes later, I fall into a hard sleep filled with dreams of Shades's rugged face buried in my muff. Shit, I can't even escape him when I'm unconscious.

Why? Why must my raging libido hold me hostage like this?

Zeppelin's "The Lemon Song" fills my ears as I climb out of my dream back to the toilet of reality. No heater running while the bus is parked. Feels as cold and empty as my apartment.

I pause the music, slide the drape aside, and peer out. "Anybody here?"

No answer. I restart the song and close the curtain.

I lie shivering on my back, staring at the steel ceiling of my too-small cage. Thoughts return to Shades, even though he's off limits.

It irks me how he blew me off. I'm not used to being ignored. Maybe because he's loaded, he thinks he's better than me.

I fucking hate entitled, rich assholes.

So why do all of my roads lead back to Todd Armstrong's Emerald Fucking City?

The way he bossed me around the night I butt-boinked him tickles the pleasure center of my brain. I expected him to submit. I liked the idea of controlling him. Humiliating him. Using him. When it backfired, it turned me on even more.

I've never had a lover top me from bottom. I'm always the one on top, even when I give up the ass. I'm the classic control freak.

Jimmy Page's solo mesmerizes me ...

I recall the feel of Shades's gorgeous tattooed spine

72

against my tits while I pounded him, the burning expression when I called him a whore … My legs shift under the thin blanket. I drag a hand over my aching breasts and rub hard, imagining his hungry mouth there. The flat of my other hand rubs my clit through the jeans in slow, sensual circles. The freezing bus isn't so cold anymore.

I unzip my pants, push them halfway down my legs, and kick off the covers.

Shades worked miracles on my pussy that night. *The tongue stud.* Jesus, the tongue stud. I close my eyes, spread my legs, and diddle my clit to the music seducing my ears. I picture his face as he stared up at me from his perch atop my mound. When he finished tongue-drilling me, he looked like he'd eaten a gourmet glazed donut.

A wave of love juices floods my basement. I slide fingertips through the thick puddle, pretending it's his glorious tongue writing me a love song. I taste myself. I fuck myself. I fall victim to memories best left forgotten.

The orgasm stalks me like a cautious predator, waiting for the right moment to spring. My finger-lanced pussy begs for release. The music rises to its climax and—

A sudden cold breeze hits my twat. Light filters through my closed lids. I open my eyes, sit straight up— or at least try to—and crack my forehead on the bunk above me.

"Fuck!" I slap a palm to my head and squint at the brightness through the dull ache.

Shades peers down at me through his trademark dark glasses, brow arched, grinning, smugger than a guilty man getting away with murder.

I yank up the blanket and rip the buds from my ears.

"Do you need a hand?" He laughs. The fucker *laughs* at me.

I'm rarely struck speechless, but I can't think of a single thing to say. I whip the curtain closed, grazing his nose in the process. He totally deserved that. And a lot more.

His laughter continues as he traipses down the aisle toward the back of the bus. Sounds of feet climbing the steps echo through the humiliation.

Oh my God, I could fucking die.

I tug my clothes into proper position and tumble out of the bed into a heap on the floor behind Shades. He turns around and looks down his punk-ass nose at me. "You *sure* you don't need a hand?"

Standing, I shoot him a bird with my wrinkled, pussy-drenched middle finger. "No, but here's a finger for you." I lick it.

His nostrils flare. "I can't wait to see Cherry Buzz Float onstage tonight."

I'm not sure if he's teasing or serious. I'll be smart and assume it's the former. Unless he's sizing up his competition ...

"Because you've never seen a real rock band? Don't worry. We'll be gentle when we pop your cherry." I pat his cheek with my masturbating hand, intentionally leaving a wet spot in his stubble.

"I prefer it rough."

"That can also be arranged." I give him my back and take one step toward the front where Jinx taps out rhythms on her drum board, and Kate is plugged into her monitor headphones, practicing. Shades's hand on my arm stops me.

"What?" I spin around and launch a barrage of eye-daggers at him.

Without a lick of emotion on his face, he shoves a white paper bag in my hands. I open it. A wrapped burger and a carton of fries. My heart skips a beat. When I look up, he's gone.

Well ...

Shit.

A LITTLE BIT HIGH, A LITTLE BIT LOW

The stage is dark. I sense fans moving below me like a colony of ants, but there's not much noise. Why aren't they screaming? My knee bounces so hard, I don't even try to stop it. This is it. This is opening night. This is the beginning of my new life.

I hope to hell I don't fuck it up.

Jinx cracks off a four-count with her drumsticks. Kate and I rip into one of our most popular songs, "No Good."

The spotlight falls on me, shocking, blinding. My heart submits to the rhythm my bass controls. The massive, rolling low notes pound, drill, and devour. Sonic booms spank the sound barrier like a naughty kid. I smile.

Thor's hammer ain't got nothing on Letty Dillinger's bass guitar.

Cheers and whistles pierce the smoke-laden club. The Rock grabs me by the tits and shakes me.

Playing in front of crowds energizes me. It's a shot of adrenaline right in the heart. The moment I mount the stage, I make the venue my bitch. I shove my mighty womancock in the place and just fuck the living fuck out of it.

Live shows void the suckage in my life, if only for an hour. When the fans bounce and dance and scream before me, I'm a goddess to be worshipped.

The music rattles the walls, the rafters, the floor—an audio dragon with breath of deafness. It's metal and leather and tattooed skin. It's raw sex with a shot of tequila. It's silk sheets set afire.

The crowd gathers closer. Fans smile up at me.

I thrust my hips, slash my Fender, and scream lyrics. My raspy voice and Kate's mad riffs complement each other. My bass rhythms syncopate with Jinx's downbeats.

Kate, Jinx, and I are components of one whole. Together, we're sweat and sound and need. We're made of the same primal instinct that drives people to feed, fuck, and fight.

Tonight, we *are* The Rock.

When "No Good" ends with Jinx catching her crashed cymbal, the crowd claps. Not nearly the welcome I hoped for, but at least they're on their feet. I scan the room through the bright lights. People of every size, shape, and color dot the pit. A girl on the left screams my name.

I laugh into the mic and will my voice to steady. "How you guys feeling tonight, Columbia?"

Shouts and appreciative whistles.

"You ready to get *fucked* by three badass bitches?" I thrust my hips to accentuate the *fuck*.

The volume rises.

I cup a hand over the back of my ear. "Sorry, what was that? You don't like getting fucked by beautiful women? That's a shame. We're horny as hell."

"Fuck us!" a guy in front yells. He's drunker than an unemployed rodeo clown. Man, I wish I were too.

I prop a combat boot on the monitor, knowing full well the boys can see up my red plaid miniskirt to the cute little lace panties underneath.

Drunkie McSkunkie rouses his nearby buddies with a chant. "Fuck us, fuck us, fuck us ..."

"Really?" Their calls reignite the hope floundering in my chest.

More join in. "Fuck us, fuck us ..."

I turn to Jinx and Kate and find some of my lost nerve. "These guys want some. Let's give them a shot of Cherry Buzz Float."

Kate nods, lifts the neck of her guitar to her lips and slides her tongue down its length. Then she tears into the opening of a new song we've been working on, "Come Crashing."

Jinx and I build the foundation with a complicated rhythm, giving and taking. The music connects us, ties us together with invisible strings. It's the most beautiful form of slavery in the world. I'm not a lesbian, but I *feel* Jinx in a way that transcends the other emotions in my repertoire. It's like we're two separate arms of the same body. If she improvises for a few beats, I never have to think about how to respond. I just do. It's perfectly natural for me. And a little fucking scary how attuned our minds are sometimes.

I could probably go lesbian for Jinx if I had to. Hell, I might already be a little—at least for the part of Jinx who sits behind the drums. But what we have isn't about sex. It's about this amazing thing we share right now. The Rock.

"When you come crashing, I'll be there," I sing. "I'll hold you up when you get scared. I'll pull you back down when you float away. When life overwhelms you, I'll open my wings. When the pain is unbearable, come crashing into me."

Endorphins raid my brain, and I lose myself in this moment of communion with my bandmates, our audience, the whole fucking universe.

My flow software engages, and I ride a wave of total immersion in time, space, and connection for the rest of the set.

We wrap up our last song to excited cheers, and I stumble out of my Rock daze. Jillian and the members of Killer Dixon watch from the side. I make a point of avoiding Shades. Now that I've rejoined the realm of reality, I'm not sure I can deal with him. Or anyone else.

"Thank you guys for coming out to support Cherry

Buzz Float tonight. Killer Dixon is up next, so refill those cups, take your pisses, and get ready to be rocked by some big ol' cocks. Good night!"

Claps and whistles take control of the airwaves as Jinx, Kate, and I depart the limelight. I make a hasty retreat backstage, dump off my bass, and rush past Shades, Rax, Toombs, and Jillian toward the fire exit.

Rax says, "Where the fuck is she going?"

"Leave it alone," Jillian replies.

The moment the night air hits my face, I bawl my eyes out. I *always* do the ugly-cry thing after landmark gigs. The music high overwhelms me. I have to let out the emotion trapped inside, or I'll explode. Jillian, Kate, and Jinx know this is part of my process from time to time, and they give me space by clearing our equipment from the stage while I work things out.

Tonight, it's different. Bittersweet emotion. The audience wasn't nearly as into the music as I was. That saddens and scares the shit out of me. Did we suck? Didn't seem like we did, but we weren't ... *there* with the crowd.

The door opens behind me.

"It's not a good idea—" A slam cuts off Jillian's voice.

"Don't worry. I'm okay, Jinx." I turn around.

Not Jinx. Shades.

Wow. Didn't see that coming.

He stands still as a statue covered in pigeon shit, staring at me through his glasses.

My skin registers the cold like an afterthought, and I wrap my arms around myself. I casually brush away the last tear, hoping he'll think I have something in my eye.

A bullet out of a gun, he hits me. We crash into the wall, a tangle of leather and plaid. He pins me to the bricks with his body and kisses me the same way he kissed my pussy the other night. Like he fucking worships me.

Uh ... what the hell?

My breath rushes as his tongue sweeps mine, its metal nub an agonizing reminder of how much my cooch misses him. Another swipe. My panties are soaked. I twist my thighs together.

Sweat from the stage evaporates off my goosebumped skin in the chilly night air. His chest crushes mine; his hard cock arches into the cradle of my hips.

I try to keep up with his mouth, but the shock of this entire scenario knocked my motor function into reboot mode. He dives in again with purpose. His fingers lift the skirt and softly rub my clit through the ruined underwear as he kisses me into the wall. I'll soon be a fucking fossil for future generations to ponder.

I gasp and push him away. My lungs heave for oxygen. My brain is still fucked up from the highs and lows of the show. I'm speechless again. Funny how he does that to me.

After a thirty-second standoff, I cross my arms over my boobs and somehow muster enough spunk to revive my charming attitude from certain death. "I thought we weren't going to do this again."

"You thought wrong." Still with the swagger, and he's not even moving. Intimidating as hell.

Gulp.

"Just because you caught me rubbing one out on the bus doesn't give you the right to—"

He snaps off his glasses and gets right up in my soul with those emerald eyes. "It's my birthday."

My heart clogs my throat. I force myself not to sputter. No fucking way. "You're full of crap."

He pulls his wallet out of his back pocket and flashes his driver's license. December 16. Sure as shit, he's a birthday boy. His hard stare bores into my head where I'm naked, and not in the good way. I don't like how he affects me. It's dangerous.

I also don't like how hurt I am that he didn't notice I

was crying.

Stupid guy.

Stupid *me* for being so ridiculously obsessed about a one-night stand I told myself meant nothing.

Refusing to shiver, despite the cold both in- and outside, I look away. I adjust my tone dial to flippant and cool. "All right. I'll give you your present tonight if you want. I did promise. Text me when you're ready."

"I don't have your number."

With a careless shrug, I say, "You're a rich boy. Put some servants on that shit."

He doesn't smile like I expect him to. He stomps to the door and goes back inside.

What a fucking dickhole.

Two can play this game. I have a PhD in dickology—giving and receiving.

I huff a deep breath. It's cold as balls out here, and not just because it's December, but I'm not going back in until he's onstage. I don't want to give him the pleasure of knowing I'm listening to him sing.

I hate him more than ever. And after that kiss, I want him so fucking badly.

Conflicted in the worst way.

I go to the bus and change into some warmer clothes, then wander around to the venue's entrance. Flashing my ID, I convince the bouncer I'm with the band, and he lets me in.

Killer Dixon is already up and running. Shades stands to the left, Rax on the right, and Toombs sits behind the drums in the middle. Their grungy song sizzles. Fans go bat-shit crazy. The air charges with The Rock's intensity. Jealousy rages within me.

Shades is a total stranger. All traces of the laid-back, cool-as-a-cucumber guy I knew have left the premises. The hot piece of rock god ass on the stage is pure sex, pure soul. He woos half-naked women at his feet, flaunting suggestive smiles between screamed lyrics, tossing them guitar picks, and serenading them. His voice ... oh fuck. If I weren't already planning to bang him tonight, I'd be sitting on a guy's shoulders flashing my tits at him right now.

The band is super tight—every note is perfect, every beat spot on, every smile perfectly engineered for maximum crowd reaction—but they still sound like every other popular hard rock band out there today. Maybe that's the attraction. Shit, I'm even enamored of Killer Dixon, and I despise them.

Fans rush the stage, waving devil horns and cell phone torches. They crawl over each other to get close. A mosh pit opens below the stage. Drunks collide into one another, tear clothing, unleash deafening screams.

Shit, I thought Cherry Buzz Float did okay tonight until these assholes came on. Is it because we're girls? Or is our sound so retro in a world of techno bullshit garbage that people can't relate to us? We churn out powerful melodies with great hooks steeped in classic, timeless rock style. What's not to love?

A crowd surfer gets tossed up and passed around on a human tsunami of excitement.

Plenty, apparently. There's no question which group the audience prefers.

My heart takes a tumble.

Goddamn it. Killer Dixon is smoking us.

I want to go home to my miserable life, my ramen noodles, and my shitty job at Fat Johnny's. Nothing is worse than thinking you're awesome, only to be put in your place by your worst enemy in front of a huge crowd.

The song wraps, and the fans go wild.

"How's it going tonight?" Shades growls into the mic. His shoulders and stance loosen. A lacy black bra lands at his feet, and several pairs of bare boobs bounce in the audience. Judging by the smile plastered on his face, he's eating up the attention. He owns every woman in this joint. The bastard.

Screams rip up the night. Shades seduces the crowd with that gorgeous smile. I throw up in my mouth a little.

"What did you guys think about Cherry Buzz Float?" He claps and nods like he's patting a good dog on the head. "Not bad, huh?" More cheers.

An indecipherable chant begins and quickly spreads. By the time the vocal wave hits the back of the room where I stand, Shades is shaking his head and laughing. He grabs a bottle of beer from the closest monitor and imbibes.

"Fuck us, fuck us, fuck us!" the women yell. Traitorous crowd. They started that shit when *we* were onstage.

"You ready for us to dive into your pants?"

"Yes!" the people holler.

"Here we go ..." Shades thrashes his bass when Toombs kicks off the next song, and he and Rax break into a hot homoerotic dueling guitar thing.

It's time to leave. I've seen enough of this shit.

I bolt out the door and wind around to the tour bus. I'd better grab a shower since I probably stink to high hell, and I'm gonna have to give up the ass to my mortal enemy in a couple hours. I could be a bitch and go skank, but I'm classier than that.

When I get to the parked behemoth, I bang on the door. Freddie startles in the driver's seat, drops his porn magazine, and lets me in.

"How'd it go?" he says, toeing the mag under his chair.

"Don't ask." I trudge to my bunk's trundle, grab supplies, and hit the shower. At least the water's warm.

How did I devolve from squatting on top of the fucking world, ready to piss on all who dare defy me to clawing my way through the underground shit pile, gasping for air?

You didn't, Letty, The Rock says.

"Rock, is that you?" I pause my hair rinsing.

Yes, it is I. You're as badass as you ever were. When shit gets you down, remember this: You're not Killer Dixon, and they're not you. You're apples and they're oranges. Both are good to different people.

So, stop comparing yourself to other bands. Stop judging yourself by someone else's standards. Stop selling yourself short.

Fuck the doubts and carry on. You were put on Earth to rock. Go forth and wow the world with your badassery. And hurry up about it.

My spirits lift. The numbness evaporates. My perspective shifts and assures me The Rock is right.

Well, of course, it's right. That's how The Rock rolls.

And tonight, I'm gonna roll all over Shades.

ANAL PROBING AND BUNK HOSING

After the show, everyone returns to the bus, high from the excitement of our debut. Rax wanted to bring chicks to bang, but Jillian told him we had to find a place to park for the night. I'm not wild about sleeping out in the open. Don't thieves target buses and RVs? It's not like we have tons to rip off, but we're hauling some expensive equipment in the trailer behind us.

Though, if we do get ripped off, Shades's daddy will probably bail us out. I glance at the birthday boy. He's back to acting like I'm invisible.

Wonder why he hasn't mentioned it's his birthday to anyone? His business. I'll leave it alone.

"Great first show, everyone." Jillian high-fives the girls and nods to the men, who are sprawled around the tables, drinking beer.

Rax clinks his bottle with Shades and Toombs. "To many more."

"You got it, man." Shades takes a sip.

Toombs stares at Jinx.

I step in front of Jinx to block his view. "You seriously rocked the skins, girl. Tomorrow let's work on a new song. I've got an idea you might like." I scavenged *most* of the bass line I scrawled on the napkin Shades stole, but a few pieces are still missing. One of the key grooves has been like a word on the tip of my tongue all day. It drives me nuts that I can't remember it.

A grin lights up her face, and Jinx nods anxiously. She fist-bumps me and follows me toward the bunks. Kate looks as pissy as ever. Still with the drama. That bitch can never be happy about anything.

Whatever.

"Ladies," Jillian calls to us.

I face her.

"Nice work tonight." No smile. No eye contact. No warmth. But coming from Jillian, it's the sweetest thing anyone's said to me all day.

"Thanks, Jillian. Good night." I climb into my bunk, clutching my cell phone, and wait.

I fall asleep.

I wake to a *buzz-ker-clunk-buzz* flopping on my chest. The text reads: *You awake?*

Holy mother loving fuck, I am now. *Who is this?* I slow type back. God, I need an upgrade. This phone sucks.

Birthday boy.

My pussy lips pucker.

Who were u thinking about when u masturbated? he says.

Why the hell does he care?

Jimmy Page. Sort of.

Liar. He knows me so well.

I'm gonna need my song back after I fuck u, thief.

Tried to give it back at restaurant. U didn't want it.

The bastard. *I changed my mind.*

U gotta win it back now.

I smother a snort with my hand. I'll bet I do. *Do u have condoms and lube?*

Yes.

R u horny? I sure hope so.

R u?

It's *your* birthday. Whatever. I don't want him to think I'm *too* gung-ho about paying him back, even though I secretly am.

Your place or mine?

I smile. *Yours.* Let him sleep on any ensuing wet spots.

I wait a solid minute to see if he types anything else. He doesn't. I peel back the curtain and look out. It's dark on the bus. Snores emanate from the front, but no sound from Kate above me. And no motor noise to drown out any stray fuck-gasps.

The challenge of keeping quiet should worry me. What worries me instead is that I don't know which bunk is Shades's. I never saw him near the beds earlier. Fuck!

Pride won't let me text him. He managed to find my phone number—I wonder who gave it to him?—so I should be able to figure out which of the three unaccounted-for bunks belongs to him.

The one directly across from me on bottom is Toombs's. Whoever's above him is snoring, so it's probably not Shades. It seems likely Freddie would sleep toward the front, and considering his size, I'm guessing he'd do better on the bottom. That means Shades is in the front top bunk.

I slip out of bed and tiptoe forward. I step on the first rung of the mini ladder and reach for the curtain. Something grabs my ankle. My heart stops for a beat, and I manage to contain the scream poised at the top of my vocal cords. I look down. Shades smiles up at me.

Jesus Christ. How did Freddie manage to get up here anyway? I step down quickly, slide into Shades's space, and slowly pull the curtain closed. It smells like him in here—that heady combination of cologne and male musk I noticed our first night together. The scent is concentrated lust.

He looks like he's about to bust a gut laughing. I cover his mouth and gaze at him through the cell phone light. His teeth playfully graze the skin on my palm.

And the juices begin to well.

Once again, I'm torn. I don't want to enjoy this. My id's writing checks my ego can't cash. Yet the promise of giving up the ass to Shades on a tour bus full of people is so fucking erotic.

Okay, enough waffling. It's time to commit and get it

over with. Where are we in the clothing department? I move my hand down his neck, stroke his throat, rub his naked chest (ooh la la!), and trail lower … oh yeah. That's what I'm talking about.

His big cock is free of restraints, and judging by the size of it, as anxious to get this show on the road as I am. I want to suck it so damn bad, but there's no room. Not unless I kneel in the aisle and lean in. Believe me, I consider it. But if we're caught, it could jeopardize the entire tour. Kate may be playing nice for the moment, but if she has the slightest inkling I've gone to "the other side," the precarious truce is as good as a hot knife through cold shit.

So, lying on my side, facing him, I palm his dick and stroke. This whole nonverbal communication thing is both annoying as fuck and rather alluring. Not knowing *exactly* what he wants for his birthday present makes it fun to guess.

He slips a hand inside my boy shorts, parts my labia, and fingers me. I want to kiss him, devour him, but I keep my desires on a leash. This is about my ass getting him off as payment for services rendered. No need to get emotionally involved.

Right?

Right.

I roll over for ease of entry and tug down the shorts. With a few kicks and a lot of wiggling, I free one leg, which is good enough. His cock bounces against my ass as I move.

Here's the thing about anal. With the right guy, it can be a lot of fun, but I've never done it with a dick this big, so I'm not sure how this is going to roll.

A thumb—I assume—rubs my clit in fast circles, thoroughly distracting me. Much as I want to come, I can't do it first. It's his birthday, after all. And there's the matter of my pride. I'm not supposed to like this guy. So,

I push his arm away and thump his man meat on my ass cheek, hoping he'll get the message.

He fidgets behind me for a few seconds, and then I hear the sound of a wrapper opening. Good. Something wet and cherry-smelling drizzles down the mound of my butt and beelines for the crack. My pussy opens like a flower in front while I spread my backside. I wish he could see me stretched wide for him. I take his index finger, swirl my tongue around it, leaving a good bit of spit behind, and guide it into my ass.

Visualizing us somewhere else where there's plenty of room and light, I release my breath gently and close my eyes. I rock my hips to give his finger better access, tighten my ass muscles, squeeze him.

His rough chest presses against my back, scratching it. His breath ruffles the hair over my ear. One hand gropes a tit while the other ass fucks me. He adjusts his angle and increases his pace. The world transforms from beautiful black and white to vivid, raging color. Oh my God, the tip of his finger hits the underside of my clit, teases that throbbing love nub slowly. The pleasure is agonizing, constricting, and freeing at the same time. Fuck, I'm gonna come.

I wrestle free of his grip. He brings the finger to his mouth and sucks my ass off it. Holy fucking Jesus.

That's it. I assume control of his lubed, condom-covered cock and spread my cheeks again. The head of his dick alone is huge, not to mention the length. I drool— literally drool—at the thought of his ten inches filling my ass.

The clit stroking resumes. Arching my back, I push my hole against his mighty wang, and open up.

The pain rips me, and I let go of a gasp. His cunt-diddling hand covers my mouth. My tongue darts out for a taste of myself, and my pussy responds with another flood. Oh my God, his cock is about to split me in two.

And I love it.

I slowly shift my hips forward. Back. A little deeper that time. Forward. Back. Deeper still. Forward. Back. He squirts more lube onto our love connection, and that's when I have a breakthrough of the erotic kind.

I take his cock—all ten inches—balls deep.

My breath rushes. I try to quiet it. I'm fucking dizzy.

Lips hit my neck, and chills climb my spine. Teeth graze as he rocks me to a new song, a Shades-and-Letty lullaby. His thrusts are gentle, perfectly timed, and Christ, his rocket rams the underside of my clit just like his finger did before. The temptation to scream his name and cut the fuck loose is too much.

Fuck the band.

I moan. He stops. Someone sighs from one of the beds. His rough hand covers my mouth again. I inhale through my nose and let out my breath slowly. We lie like that, with his dick fully engaged in my backfield for several minutes.

The waiting is agony. I want more of him. I need him moving, taking, imbibing. I remember the taste of his cum on my tongue in the hotel room, the rapturous expression after I finished with him, the way we passed out afterward.

Much as I don't want to admit it, he's my sexual soul mate. No inhibitions. No fear. No boundaries.

And tomorrow I have to go back to pretending I don't give a shit.

He uncovers my mouth and resumes his gentle thrusts to the pulse of my throbbing clit. I'm spread as wide as the small space allows. Vulnerable. Naked. I should hate him for forcing my hand with the birthday vow, but I could have refused, and I didn't. I guess that says a lot about me.

I draw up my bent legs to give him wider access, and his thrusts roughen. He yanks my face toward his and goddamn it, he stares at me while he fucks my asshole into oblivion. Lips fall on mine, softer than I expect. His tongue eases inside my mouth, stroking with that delicious silver stud.

I finger fuck myself. My clit screams for release. My ass burns with fever. *Come on, motherfucker, make me come.* I put my hips into it and assume control of the thrusts, impaling myself over and over on his glorious rod the same way he did when roles were reversed. He squeezes my tits so hard, these bitches will probably have bruises tomorrow. Still kissing me, he pauses a second as his lower half halts all forward movement. I can only assume he's filling that rubber. Goddamn it, what a waste of good cum.

I rejoice in knowing I made him climax first. Now it's time for me to pay the piper. Squeezing my ass tight around his schlong, I ride him for three more strokes. The head of his cock hits my clit like a battle ram, and sweet Jesus, Mary, and Joseph, I douse the fucking curtain with my release.

I fucking squirt.

Never done that before.

In the aftermath, I quietly heave for breath. Shit, he had to have noticed. Is he thoroughly disgusted?

He reaches around me and touches the wet fabric drape. He licks his fingers, and the rest of me melts. I want to see if I can do it again. Maybe I'll aim for his face next time. Cunt hydrant. Fuck!

I feel his grin in the dark. His arms enclose me in a blanket of cum and warmth and satisfaction. And then he kisses me. Not like a guy who's flailing in wild throes of passion. Not like a guy motivated purely by sex. Not like a guy trying to shut me up and get rid of me. No, his tongue makes love to my mouth. Slow, careful circles floating on waves of desire. Without thinking, I answer with the same warmth.

Then my brain crashes the party.

Do not get involved. This is the last stop for you and him. Time to get off the train and make a clean break. You honored your promise. Now get the fuck out of his bed and don't come back.

Yeah. Like that's gonna happen after he made me hose his bunk.

But I really should leave. I don't want him assuming this is more than payback, even though it's starting to shape up that way.

Fuck. Why do I always fall for guys who are totally wrong for me? Tomorrow, he'll probably act like nothing ever happened. When he gets horny and can't find a groupie to bang, he'll come looking for another bash-and-dash.

But would that be so bad? And who says I can't use him the same way? If we agree to keep it casual and not get involved beyond the fucking, we both win.

I like this plan.

I pull his still-hard honey dipper from my ass, and he sighs. I use his bed sheet to sop up the stray squirt juice that got on my leg and to tidy up the lube on my ass. I drag my little shorts up, peek past the curtain, and survey. Coast is clear. He touches my arm and lifts a brow. With a saucy grin, I leave him with the mess and commando crawl to the bathroom to clean up any remaining fluids.

See, it was a good idea to do it at his place after all. I'm so pleased.

Once I settle in my bed, my phone vibrates.

U made me so hard tonight, he says.

Ass fucking does that 2 a guy.

No. When u were onstage.

I shut my open mouth with the flat of my hand. He liked watching me play? Maybe that's what the "attack" after Cherry Buzz Float's set was about. Fuck, that's an even bigger turn-on than the squirting was.

Can I have my song now?

No.

Smug, rich bastard. Why am I not surprised? Though playing fuck-tag with him to try and win the napkin back could be a hell of a lot of fun. The perfect carrot to dangle in front of me.

Footsteps trudge down the aisle toward me. My pulse takes off at a sprint. I squint through the crack in the drape. Damn it, Shades doesn't even pause as he passes my bunk. He must be going to the bathroom.

Maybe he's thinking the same thing I am. That we can keep up the steamy-hot sex as long as we don't get caught.

The possibilities boggle. And the possibility of being discovered at any moment ratchets up my need for variety. Ah, the glorious temptation of pretending to hate Shades in front of the band but secretly fucking his brains out at every opportunity gets the juices flowing anew.

I'm officially in love with this plan.

This is going to be the beginning of a beautiful partnership.

INTERLEWD TWO

It turns out undercover fucking does wonders for inspiration. I spend the next few days working on songs with Kate and Jinx. I ignore Shades, as he does me.

At least in public. Nobody knows we've been texting each other on and off. He sends daily sweet little ditties like, *I dreamed I tied u facedown on a bed of hundred-dollar bills and drilled u.* Or *I wanna drizzle your ass cheeks with cum.* Or my favorite, *I miss your pussy, pussycat.*

Isn't he a doll?

The interaction and ensuing sexual tension fucking rock, except for the fact that my phone is a hunk of dinosaur dung, and it takes me ten minutes to reply. By the time I shoot off my return message into cyberspace, the hotness of the moment has passed.

Ah, well. At least our illicit communications provide vivid fantasy stimulation while I'm churning my butter alone in my bunk at night.

I try not to think about the phone charges my mom's gonna have to pay this month. Fuck it. I've been pretty good about keeping my activity to a minimum until now.

First on my wish list when Cherry Buzz Float makes it big: a smartphone.

"Let's take a quick break. I need to refuel," I say after a two-hour marathon session. "This song has a lot of potential if we can just nail down the chorus."

Kate nods. "Yeah, we're close."

I love it when the three of us get into the same headspace.

I pull out my trundle and fish around for a protein bar.

Jillian grabs the hot pot and turns it on. "I don't think I've seen you eat real food since we got on this bus."

From the back, Shades catches my eye for a split second, and then looks away. Jillian's almost right. Shades gave me the burger and fries on our first day, and he's been leaving me other stuff here and there. Yesterday, I found a wrapped sandwich and a bag of chips in my bunk. No note. No comment. But I knew it was Shades.

I appreciate the sentiment, but it makes me feel weird. Like I owe him something.

And it's awkward texting him my thanks. I'd much rather do it in person—maybe even ask him to stop taking pity on me, though I'm flattered he thinks of me—but we haven't had a second to ourselves. Kate's ever watchful. Rax stays up drinking until all hours and sleeps in, which makes responding to booty calls damn near impossible. Although Jillian put her foot down and had a "come to Jesus" meeting with him yesterday, so maybe I'll get some tonight.

I read the ingredients on the protein bar package. "Says here it's got one hundred percent of my recommended daily allowance for every-fucking-thing." I take a bite of the cardboard-textured delicacy and hide a wince.

Jillian scoops instant coffee into a mug. "You can't live off that shit, Letty. You gotta eat real food every once in a while."

I shrug and gobble down the rest of my lunch. I start to ask when we'll get paid, but if I do it now, it'll be too obvious that I'm in desperate need of cash. I'll wait until I can get Jillian alone. Most of the shows have had pretty good turnouts. I assume we'll get some decent bank soon. Not that Shades needs the money. But I'd feel a hell of a lot better if I could afford my own burgers. Still, it's nice that he cares. Or at least pretends to.

"I gotta have some pussy tonight." Rax rubs his cock

absently. "How 'bout we stop off at a strip club after the show? We'll pick up some ass, do our thang, and then get on the road."

Kate looks up. "You are *not* bringing skank-hos on this tour bus to fuck."

"If the bus is a skank-ho-free zone, then you'll have to leave too, Kate," Rax says.

"Rax." Jillian's threatening tone deflects Kate's volcanic reaction.

"Come on, Jillian." Rax tosses up a hand. "I'm used to fucking two or three women a day. If I don't lay some pipe soon, I might lose my motivation. And you can't afford that."

Jillian stirs her coffee. "There are other people on the bus to consider, asshole. I don't want to hear you banging girls, either."

"Then we need a system to let everyone know when fuckery abounds." Rax tosses up a peach and catches it.

"Put up a fucking sign. 'Gang bang in progress. Do not disturb.' Easy enough." Toombs snatches the thrown peach before it hits Rax's waiting hands and takes a bite. Juice runs from the side of his mouth.

Goddamn, there's something about a bad boy. If I weren't already in lust with Shades, I'd take Toombs for a test drive. I flick a glance to Shades, but my gaze collides with Jinx. She's staring at Toombs.

Oh fuck. She better not be thinking about getting involved with him. He'll mop the floor with her and throw her in a dumpster when he's done.

Wait a minute. Did Toombs say, "gang bang"? Shit, maybe the rumors are true.

Double shit. Jinx *definitely* doesn't need to get interested in that shit.

After Kate and Rax broke up, I heard Rax, Danny, and Toombs had taken to tag-teaming girls. Rax would set up everything—find the chicks, sweet talk them, and seduce them. Then the other two would come on the scene, do their business, and make a quick getaway. They left cleanup to Rax. He's twisted and likes to fuck with girls' minds. They say the three of them were inseparable in the bedroom. I didn't believe it until now.

The way Toombs always defaults to Rax confirms it. I wonder what kind of fucked-up relationship those two have. Are they bi? Definitely not gay. I admit I'd love to find out. As a vicarious observer, of course.

Well …

Okay, *maybe* as a victim, but only if Shades got involved too.

What am I thinking? A foursome with the evil triumvirate of Killer Dixon?

The twat dam opens and liberates a few droplets of liquid sex from the gates. I look down. I have on a miniskirt with no underwear, and vagina batter is dripping down my thighs. Great.

Bathroom break.

I rush to the toilet and clean up. This tour is gonna do my head in. I'm so fucking horny, I could hump the toilet paper roll. And now that I have an image in my head of doing Shades, Rax, and Toombs on the couch, my concentration is officially balls.

My phone vibrates.

While they r occupied with groupies tonight, I'll fuck u against the bus outside.

Matching screams with Rax's and Toombs's scores? I choke on the sudden glut of spit in my mouth.

How can we be sure they won't look out? Or that Jillian, Kate, or Jinx won't see us?

No guarantees. Which is why I have to do it. The thrill of knowing someone could discover us at any moment will make the experience even hotter.

Sweet fucking Sally.

I'm in, I type back.

GANG BANG IN PROGRESS: DO NOT DISTURB

Though Cherry Buzz Float got off to a rough start on this tour, each show is better than the last. The crowd tonight is twice as big as any of the other gigs we've played so far, but I still don't feel we've had a breakthrough yet. Killer Dixon, on the other hand, makes us look like amateurs. I can't figure it out. And worse, Jinx tells me they're almost a thousand likes ahead of us on our fan pages. We seriously need a new strategy. I won't be stood up by second-rate rockers, no matter how fucking good they are in bed.

I watch Killer Dixon side stage for a few minutes and sink my eye-darts into Shades's ass. The way he moves under the lights is the same way he moves when we fuck. A master of motion, a manipulator of pleasure switches, a collector and breaker of hearts. Totally fucking hot. He may be all about his fans right now, but I'll make him forget them soon enough. God, I could come just thinking about what he's gonna do to me in an hour.

Kate jostles me out of my reverie. "Freddie says there's no strip club near here, but there are tons in Jacksonville—our next stop." Kate scowls at the band. "Fair warning."

"Maybe while they're trolling the titty aisles, we can use their absence to our advantage," I suggest. "We're booked for two nights in Jacksonville, right?"

She nods, her expression not eager but downright conniving. "What do you have in mind?"

"While the boys pick up chicks after the show tomorrow, we'll campaign for ourselves outside the strip club. Flash a little leg, jiggle some boobs, and getting the likes we need will be child's play."

"Good plan." Kate pops her gum. It may be the first time I've seen Kate smile since the tour started.

"Jinx, you with us?"

The drummer balances her gaze between Kate and me, and then nods.

"Rock on."

The guys wrap up their set, and Jillian flutters over, looking a little rattled. God, is that a misplaced hair on her head? Methinks so.

"I just found out management promised the local radio station a meet-and-greet after the show," Jillian says. She looks like she needs a cigarette.

"You're shitting me," I say.

"Nope. Be on your best behavior, and let's meet some fans."

Fuck yes! This is what rock 'n' roll is all about.

Sure enough, a few minutes later, some chicks enter the room and head for the sweaty guys eating up a big chunk of backstage real estate. Ranging in age from about eighteen to twenty-five, the women flit around Killer Dixon, squawking and gawking.

Where are the male fans?

A blond bimbo sidles up to Shades, slithers her arm around him, and poses for a picture. She's all tits and ass, and he's totally checking her out. Heat sears up my neck to my face. The flash goes off. She doesn't let go. Shades smiles and chats her up. Oh, hell no. Bitch better get her hands off my man. I start over their way. I'm taking this girl down.

Wait a minute.

I stop midstep. Shades doesn't belong to me any more than I belong to him. Just because he sends me those adorable sexts every day doesn't mean he wants me for anything else. I gotta put a lid on my rage and remember we're not dating, we're not exclusive, and we certainly don't care about each other.

Nobody can know I'm jealous as hell—least of all, Kate.

I grit my teeth and smile like a good girl.

Chitchat ensues, and Killer Dixon eats up the attention. Rax sits on a couch surrounded by barely dressed women. He has one on each knee, and two on either side. They're like pimp accessories—all shiny and flashy. Judging by the looks he's giving his groupie harem, feeding the lust is his prime objective. No problem there. Hell, he might even bag all six of them.

Toombs stands off to the side watching Rax like a hungry hawk. He takes an occasional sip of beer. A couple of girls start to approach him but back off when he looks their way. They *should* be afraid.

Then there's Shades. Girls pet his fauxhawk, pinch his ass, press their knockers against him. I keep expecting him to look my way, but he's too wrapped up in his newfound notoriety to notice me.

I stomp my foot. "Where are *our* fans?"

Kate shakes her head and keeps quiet.

Jinx watches Toombs from the shadows, and I feel a little bad for her. But it's for the best that he goes on the prowl for someone else. He would *break* her. Jinx deserves a nice guy who'll treat her like a queen.

A fresh batch of fans enters, and a few of them wander over our way. I put on my fake smile and thank them for coming to see us. A friendly, shoot-the-shit chat reveals they're Killer Dixon fans.

Why doesn't anyone care about Cherry Buzz Float, goddamn it?

Fuck my life.

The meet-and-greet goes on for an hour. One of the DJs from the local radio station interviews Shades and Rax. Toombs wants nothing to do with it. I flash a hopeful smile at the DJ when he wraps up with Killer Dixon. He smiles back and packs up his shit.

Seriously?

This. Fucking. Sucks.

By the time the place starts to clear, my stomach is in knots, and I've lost my sexual appetite. I glance to the couch where the guys sit. I'm totally off Shades's radar. Along with everyone else's, apparently.

"I'm going to get a drink," I tell the girls. Screw my highly limited cash stash. Surely, we'll get paid soon. I grab my shit, exit the stage door, and hit the bar.

The bartender tells me he likes my voice and gives me a free martini. At least there's that. I guess I am a little bit lucky about some things. Though, getting lucky with Shades tonight doesn't seem like much of a possibility anymore.

I'm so pissed right now. Not only can I not get laid, but my preferred layer keeps upstaging me at every opportunity. Fuck this shit.

I finish my drink, thank the bartender, and return backstage. Jillian, Kate, and Jinx are discussing some issues with the new song. The members of Killer Dixon are nowhere in sight.

I gesture to the empty couch. "Where'd everybody go?"

Kate rolls her eyes. "Guess."

Fuck. Me. "The bus."

"You got it, sister."

Donkey cocks humping a dump truck's junk.

I engineer an apathetic expression while swallowing the bile climbing my throat. "Just as well. I met a guy in the bar," I lie. "He wants to take me to his car for a quick boot-knocking. I'll meet you on the bus in an hour."

"I hope you have condoms," Jillian calls as I rush through the exit.

It's not like I'll need them tonight.

The polar temperature bites hard into my tits, and my scrawny blubber layer loses the fight against the cold. I stand in the back parking lot, shivering, scowling at the bus across the blacktop. That motherfucker.

Even though my head urges me to forget about it, my heart has to know. I plod over to the bus, my feet filled with the lead of dread.

So what? It's not like you own his body. You have a rental agreement at best. If he wants to bang other chicks, it's his prerogative. As long as he's being safe.

Right. Safety is a good cover for jealousy. I'll use that.

When I get to the bus, I hide in the shadows and listen to the shenanigans inside.

"Yeah, baby, suck that cock." Rax growls. "And you Blondie, play with my balls while you jerk off Toombs."

Muffled, presumably wang-stuffed female grunts escape through a cracked window. Rhythmic banging accentuates their moans.

Where the hell is—

Shades appears beside me and clamps his hand over my mouth, as he's so fond of doing. Well, this time, it was a good idea. I guess I have a tendency to shriek when he surprises me.

He holds his index finger over his lips and leads me by the hand to the back end of the bus.

"You thought I was in there." He grins that sexy grin that makes me want to shoot strawberries like a love cannon from my cooch.

"So, what if you were?" I blow off the insinuation, even though I want to slap his face.

He steps into my personal space and guides me to the other side of the bus. There's a nice big wall there. No one can see us unless they come looking. Fuck, my pulse hammers in my veins.

"I'd finish my girl off and come out to find you."

Grr … "We're not having sex again until you promise

103

you'll use condoms with the other chicks you fuck."

He holds up his right hand. "If I fuck another woman, I swear I'll wear a condom."

Then I remember he's adventurous. "Or another guy."

He shakes his head. "Or another guy. Can we get on with it now?"

So, he doesn't deny he might fuck another guy. Intrigue beats some of my anger into submission.

I close the gap between us. My hands skate up to his leather-covered shoulders. "Where'd your groupie go?" Vapor swirls between us in the cold.

"I gave her to Rax and Toombs."

"Why?"

"Not my type."

I refuse to read anything into his answer, but I utter a silent *Huzzah!* "Why didn't you tell anyone it was your birthday the other day?" Not sure why it bugs me that he celebrated his special day much the same as I did mine: without fanfare.

He grasps my open coattails and tugs me close enough to feel the rigid dick straining beneath his jeans. His green eyes spark in the shadows. An onslaught of quim quivers seizes me.

"Because I don't want to be treated differently from anyone else," he says.

Huh. I figured Daddy's boy would expect the world to bow down and worship him and his gold on his birthday. Maybe it's a macho guy thing not to make a big deal over birthdays.

"Are we gonna talk all night?" he asks.

He doesn't have to tell me twice. "Ah, no. We can absolutely get to the fucking now."

Grinning, I unbutton and unzip his jeans. No underwear to prevent his monster trouser snake from rearing its head to strike. I lick my lips and then drag them over the head of his cock while staring up at him. His eye contact assures me he's with me and not someone else, like that groupie who was all over him. I savor it.

Teasing, sucking, tasting, I take him deep. He grabs my head and fucks my hungry mouth. The fluid beading at the tip of his cock kisses the back of my throat. I provide a little hint of teeth every few strokes to let him know I'm in charge. He defies me by pulling out and beating my lips with his magic muscle.

I spit on the head and spread the natural lube with my fingers. It's a weird sensation, cold spit on a hot rocket, but I like it. I draw my tongue up and down the underside of his shaft. His head tips against the bus as he hisses a long inhale. His hips return to the game and thrust harder into my mouth.

Shades has the most glorious dick.

Clutching his length with both hands, I suck his balls one at a time. They're fucking huge. No way I can accommodate both at once, though I try anyway. As soon as I secure one and open wider for the other, the first one tumbles out. It's a fun challenge. Even better when I moan around a mouthful. The vibrations must tickle because he executes a full-body shiver.

I stand and fondle his sac. "I want these nuts slapping my clit."

Grinning, he spins me around and shoves my cheek against the wall. The miniskirt lifts. My bare ass is freezing, but I have a feeling things are about to heat up.

He leans over my shoulder as fingers part and penetrate my pussy lips. "Soon. I've been jonesing for another taste of your cunt for days. Maybe I can get you to spray my face like you did my curtain."

Now it's my turn to shiver, and it ain't because of the cold. A flood of melted muff butter leaks down my legs, and I moan long and hot. My thighs quiver, lose their strength, and I wobble in his arms. "I'll do my best. I've never squirted like that before. I wouldn't mind trying again."

I shouldn't have confessed that. It gives him too much power, but I'm so weak from the pounding of his heart against my spine, the warmth of his breath, and the thought that eating me out might give him even a tenth of the pleasure I get out of giving him head.

Shit. Am I falling for Shades? Or is this just an insanely intense sexual thing?

It's one hundred percent sexual.

At least I think it is until I turn in his arms and caress his rough cheek. His devious gaze bores through me, straight into my woman bits. The pleasure fans out from there, on a collision course with my heart.

I don't know anything about this guy.

"Give me five minutes with your pussy." His middle finger still deep inside me, he squares his shoulders. Determination and commitment flare in his eyes. He withdraws and sucks the finger like a Popsicle. Even employs sound effects.

Female screams emanate from inside the bus, followed by male grunts. Laughter. A slap.

Oh God, I could almost come now. "I'll give you three minutes. Then I'm taking control of the situation."

"You've got a deal, pussycat." He drops to his knees. I lift my combat-booted foot and hook a leg around his broad shoulders. Using a combination of tongue and hand, he muff dives, stroking and sucking my clit while curling two fingers inside me. He pumps his arm fast and hits me straight in the G-spot I didn't know I had.

"Fuck, fuck, fuck …" I mumble. He pins my back and arms against the wall. His head's under my skirt, cock jutting straight up from his open jeans. I twist my hair into a thick, red rope and bite down on it to keep from screaming his fucking name to the stars.

The cold flips my tits on high beams, but my skin is on fire. Beads of sweat bloom all over me.

"Yes! Yes! Yes!" A woman inside screeches. The bus rocks. Sounds like an animal dying a slow, torturous death in there.

I tighten my grip around Shades as his tongue plunges in and out of my cunt. Another finger gets in on the action. There have to be at least three fucking me now. At this point, I'm pretty sure I can take the whole fist.

"I'm gonna come," Rax yells. "Open wide, baby." A long, drawn-out groan follows. "Ah, fuck me ..." More grunts. "Yes, swallow that shit down, girl ..."

I twist away from Shades, grab him by the ears, and pull him up. "Fuck me, Shades. Fuck me until I come like Rax did."

He arches a brow and reaches into his leather jacket pockets. One hand produces a small bottle of lube. The other comes up empty. He hesitates. "Shit. I left the condoms inside the bus."

The moment of truth stalks me. Beads of cum roll down my legs in earnest. If I don't get off in the next five minutes, I'll fucking die.

I lick my lips. "Are you clean? Tell me the truth." He said he was the night we met, but I have to be sure.

"As far as I know."

That doesn't sound promising. "You always safe?"

"Unless I'm in a relationship, yeah."

My heart stumbles out of rhythm. "I really want to fuck you bareback, but—"

"Then let's do it. I trust you. You on birth control?"

"Yes, but—"

"You don't trust *me*." His expression loses a lumen of intensity.

He's right. I don't trust him. I have every reason not to.

But maybe I should.

I turn around, slide up my skirt, and present my ass for his viewing pleasure. I'm one big raw nerve, a ball of conflicted emotion. The ultimate "fuck you" would be to walk away and leave him with blue balls. Let him find another chick to screw. This is the perfect opportunity to cut my enemy loose for once and for all.

I meet Shades's gaze over my shoulder. God, I shouldn't do this. "Take me. However you want. Just fuck me."

A squeal penetrates the night as the bus starts rocking again. Giggles follow.

"I was hoping you'd say that." He grins, licks his hand, pumps his cock, and spears my pussy.

I throw my head back and bite off the "fuck" on the tip of my tongue. I grind my hips, twist, and shake. Riding him like a corkscrew, I let go of my inhibitions and embrace the crazy ride, accept it like a gift left on my altar.

"That's it. Milk my cock, pussycat," he breathes in my ear, and his lips skip down the steamed column of my neck.

"Yes, God, yes." Without a condom, it's better than I dreamed. He's so gonna screw me over. I'll blame my poor decision-making on a genetically driven lack of impulse control and hope for the best.

"You fantasized about me when I caught you playing with yourself on the bus. Didn't you, Letty?"

I love it when he says my name. I hate it when he reads my mind. "Yes."

I reach inside my coat, under my shirt, and yank my bra up. I clamp one of his hands on my tit, and he kneads it.

His other hand slides around front and rubs my clit. "I'm gonna fill up this sweet little box with hot Toddy."

I giggle.

My pussy is a dripping, dick-pumped well. A milky river flows down my legs. "My ass, Shades. Do my ass like you did the other night on the bus. I wanna spray this fucking wall with cum graffiti."

"I'll lick it off the goddamn bricks," he whispers in my ear.

Fuuuck …

He pauses for a moment. My legs tremble at the sudden lack of friction. Something cold squirts and drips into my crack. Once I'm properly greased, I pull him out of the front and shove his rod through the back door. A cry escapes me. I can't help it. At this point, I don't care if anyone sees us. In fact, that might turn me on even more. Bring it, motherfuckers.

His girth fills me, stretches me to the point of ripping. I need this agonizing pleasure so badly. Need him.

"Letty … Jesus Christ, you're a wild fucking beast." He grabs me by the hair and pulls me backward to look at his sweaty red face. Our lips fall into kissing range, but there's no contact. Ravenous lust steeps his expression. And a smidge of something else. Respect?

Ah, fuck. I never considered I might serve as anything more than a base sexual fantasy to him. Goddamn it, I like it. I laugh out loud. The endorphin rush makes me.

"Is tonight's performance good enough to win back my song?" I tighten my rectal muscles on his next lunge, and he growls.

"Pretty fucking close." He releases my hair and gropes my throat. His hand squeezes, cutting off a little air. My pulse races in reply, and I step up the heat by meeting his heavy thrusts halfway.

"Fuck it, girl," Rax says. He must've opened the window all the way. It almost sounds like he's right here with us.

"Yeah, fuck it," I tell Shades. "Fuck it like you'll never have it again. Fuck it like you hate it." My butt cheeks bounce and breaths strain with his brutal poundings. "Make my ass beg for more."

Goddamn it, he does. I'm lost in a haze of lust and hot skin and bodily fluids. Drowning, choking, dying for more. Control ebbs away, and pure chaos descends. I fucking love this.

"I want a taste." Rax materializes out of thin air beside us, and I almost shit all over Shades's cock.

"Oh my fucking God!" I disengage and grab my chest. Breaths rush on a collision course with hyperventilation. My heart trips over itself. "Oh my God."

Shades stares at Rax as if he wants to rip the guy's head off. "What the fuck, man?"

Shit, we are so busted. I smooth my skirt to cover the mess we've made down below. Motherfuck.

Rax leans against the bus and studies us. The howls and rocking continue inside. Rax must've left Toombs to finish off the ladies.

"Shades and Letty. Didn't see that coming." He steps closer and glances at Shades's swollen dick saluting him. "But I'd like to."

"We just got a little drunk—"

"How about a three-way, and I won't tell Kate." With the top of his hair pulled into a ponytail on the back of his head, Rax looks like a sleazy car salesman, which is kind of a twisted turn-on.

Shades says nothing.

"You wouldn't dare tattle." I'm reaching for any excuse to deny what my libido demands: exactly what Rax's offering. It's so wrong, yet I'm so worked up, I can't help wanting it.

Mixed signals fire in my brain. Rax is a total fucking ass munch. Why the hell am I remotely considering anything sexual with him? Because I'm a masochist with an insatiable appetite for sex and trouble. Not necessarily in that order.

I try to redirect Rax. "Telling Kate would ruin the tour."

He lifts a brow. "For you, maybe."

Eyes narrowed, Shades focuses on Rax. Protective.

Territorial. Also hot.

My mind races. The two of them. Together. Behind the bus. Making a muffaletty sandwich.

I sweep my gaze down Rax's front. Nice big bulge in the trousers. Sculpted six-pack under the tight T-shirt. Tattoos and piercings galore. He may be a cunt, but his body is fucking badass as hell. I can overlook idiocy for the sake of an amazing orgasm and a taboo thrill ride.

I know I'll regret this tomorrow, but I want to fuck Shades and Rax.

"You got protection?" I say.

Shades snaps his neck my way. I expect a confrontation with disappointment, but he's grinning. The pervert wants to do it too?

Score!

Rax holds up a wrapped condom. "Liquor in the front or poker in the rear?"

I smile at his joke. *I* get to tell *them* what to do? Oh, hell yes.

"I've had quite enough licking, but I wouldn't mind being filled with two big dicks at once." I glance at Rax's zipper.

He unleashes his beast, which rivals Shades's in length, but he's a little bigger around. Perfect for feeding this starving cum catcher.

Rax rolls the condom over his shaft and strokes it. Holy fuck, is that …? Shit. It is. Kate was right. The snake tattoo slithering up his neck really does end at the tip of his cock. Jesus Christ, how much booze did he have to drink to sit through a couple of hours of dick needle torture?

I'll have to marvel over that one some other time. I've got a date with double penetration first …

I can't believe I'm fucking doing this. And Shades seems all in. Standing behind me, he wraps his arms protectively around my waist—which makes me even hotter—and dives back into my ass with no warning.

This standing angle is a new one. I lose my breath for a few strokes as Rax watches Shades fucking my hole. God, the blend of pleasure and pain is exquisite. In and out he pumps while I finger myself. I hold up my hand for Rax to taste. He sucks my flavor off.

Next thing I know, my shirt is up, and he's suckling my tit. "God, yeah." I clutch his face harder against my nipple. "Suck it, Rax. Suck it while Shades fucks my ass. Don't you wish it was you in there?"

"Bitch." Rax's dick stroking picks up speed. Shades pounds me harder, bites my neck. Rax fingers me.

I slap his hand away. "No, you cunt drip. Put your dick in my pussy. And stare at Shades while you fuck me."

Shades's breath heaves. Rax's smile suggests he's found heaven. I aim to ensure we all arrive at the Pearly Gates at the same time. Preferably with him in my mouth.

The male dynamic is fascinating. If Shades was horny before, he must've sprouted about a dozen more balls now. He's an apex predator who knows he can't lose. I can't wait to see his reaction to sharing me with his bandmate.

I grab Rax's cock and slide it in. Sweet fucking Jesus, he's big. I have to stand on tiptoes to give them both the angle they need. I wobble. Rax comes to the rescue and lifts me off the ground. I sling my legs tight around his thighs and ride him like a kid in a bouncy chair. Shades's dick slams my ass in sync. I feel both men ramming each other from the inside. God, they must be enjoying this almost as much as I am.

Rax stares at me with a wicked grin. I slap his face. "I said look at Shades, motherfucker."

He drives harder—probably in retaliation—but his gaze shifts to Shades.

"Now kiss him."

The grin widens. Rax tears into Shades, who pauses his

thrusts for a moment. Their eyes close and tongues mingle. I'm grateful for the break in the action. If they hadn't stopped, I'd have hosed Rax down like a mud wrestler after a match.

After an erotic display, their lips separate. I lick both sets of lips, and our kisses become a communal one. Three tongues, three passions feeding one body: mine. Rax diddles my clit, and I squeeze my ass around Shades again. He moans into the tangle of mouths. I stroke Shades's cheek beside my head. "That was so fucking hot."

Crushed between them, I buck my hips and restart the dick engines. "Now, who wants to come first?"

"After you, pussycat," Shades says.

"What a gentleman. I, on the other hand, am not." Rax hefts me up and readjusts his hold. I lean into his chest to give Shades a better angle for ass pounding. And pound he does. Seems as though Rax's appearance has given his cock renewed energy.

"Well, then, Rax gets to come on my face while Shades watches."

Rax lowers my feet to the ground and pulls out. He whips off the condom and tosses it aside. Shades's pork sword keeps the back door rocking. I bend over and take Rax's cock in my mouth while Shades slows his pace for several beats, then pulls out. I smile around the meat in my mouth. Shades almost lost it that time.

I drop to my knees at Rax's feet.

Rax strokes my hair as I suck the life out of him. He smooths it, cups my chin, stares into my eyes. "I'm ready to blow, Letty."

I swirl my tongue around his shaft once more and smile. White cum spurts across my teeth. I dart out my tongue to catch his falling raindrops.

"Uhh," he groans as he coaxes the last of his load onto my face.

I flash him and Shades the glob of spank sauce on my tongue, swallow, and open wide. Then I rub some of the jizz that missed my mouth into my cheek, trail it down to my tongue, and suck it off my fingers. "Mmm, so fucking good."

Rax squeezes the head of his dick and shakes it at me. "Goddamn, girl."

I shift my gaze to Shades behind me, who's leashed the head of his cock with a tight fist. "Your turn."

"You first."

"I insist." I need him on me, coating me.

I get to my feet. Rax stares at me, dick in palm, pumping the fucker. He's had at least two orgasms in the last twenty minutes, and now he's ready for round three? That guy must be the machine everyone says he is. He'll make some girl lucky one day.

But as hot as he is, he's not for me.

I face Shades. He winds his arms around my used body and kisses me long and deep. Does he taste Rax's cum tingling my tongue? If so, he doesn't seem to care. God, this man is uh-fucking-mazing. He puts his whole upper body into the lip lock, submerses me, consumes me with waves of passion and possession.

Shades covets me.

Something clicks inside and sets off all kinds of alarms in my head. He's getting too close. I break away and swipe my mouth with the back of a hand.

Shaking off the feeling of falling, I bend over, turn my head, and toss over my shoulder to Shades, "Fuck my ass, then add your cum to Rax's. All over my face. Understand?"

A shaft up the bum is the only answer I get. My beautiful rock star thrusts to a silent rhythm, and I catch the beats in my head. Closing my eyes, I concentrate on the subatomic music we make together. The notes seep into my crevices and penetrate down to my soul. This is greater than any high, any drug, any addiction. It's pure and raw.

A pair of hands push me to a vertical position. My lids snap open. Rax kneels before me, hugs my thighs, and supports some of my weight. He buries his face in my pussy while Shades rocks my ass. It's an awkward angle to accommodate, so I widen my stance, spreading open my knees while sticking out my butt for Shades. Rax lowers his head so he's directly under me, in perfect view of both my cream-dripping cooch and Shades's dick giving my hole what for.

His tongue swipes my clit, draws circles inside and traces the lines of my labia. His bird finger penetrates me, and I sense the other ones bumping Shades's balls. Bumps turn into caresses, and Shades moans. My clit swells to the point of pain.

"Lick his sac," I tell Rax.

Shades pauses his thrusts.

My back to his chest, I curl an arm around his neck and draw his lips to mine. Rax's cum is nearly dry. "Do it for me?" Saying those words is a huge gamble. They assume a lot.

Shades doesn't reply. But he also doesn't protest. He resumes slow, gentle surges that light up my insides. The acknowledgment of my needs at the possible denial of his own isn't lost on me. Shades just took this "relationship" to a new level.

I look down at Rax fondling my nether lips. "Lick him."

And he does. His tongue darts out to greet each of Shades's ingresses, and I watch from my awkward perch with fascination. Shades is letting his bandmate lick his balls while he fucks my ass. Sex has never been so hot.

Thrusts speed up. Pressure builds. Shades's magic schlong finds the sweet spot behind my clit.

Rax's tongue is everywhere at once. On my pussy. My

nub. Shades's balls and even his shaft as it pounds my ass. No inhibitions within a twenty-foot radius.

Bang. Suck. Bang. Slurp. Bang. Gobble, gobble.

Somehow Shades's cock gets harder, penetrates deeper.

The cold air, the grassy scent of dried cum on my face, and the sounds of Rax licking balls converge into one massive sensory overload.

Shades pushes Rax out of the way and steps in front of me. His brows pull together, his lips part to reveal those scandalous, perfect white teeth, and he nails me with a devoted stare that bisects my soul.

"Give me that hot white cum, Shades. I wanna swallow your essence. Make it mine." I open my mouth to accept his gift.

Rax watches with an awed expression.

Shades lets fly a muffled declaration of apparent pleasure between clenched teeth, along with enough cum to fill my mouth. The stuff shoots under my eye, across the bridge of my nose, and runs down the corners of my lips. His salty-bitter taste emblazons my mind. I desperately swallow, wanting more. I grab his cock and suck it. His legs tremble as I coax the last few stubborn drops out of him. He falls against the wall, looking dazed for several seconds.

I smear his jizz over my skin as I did with Rax's. I lick my lips, smile, and kiss him softly for a long moment. The music in my head continues to play. He's now a part of it. His "voice" harmonizes with mine. A chill catches me, and I shiver.

He finds my aching nub and thumbs it. Pressing his forehead to mine, he says, "You didn't come."

I smile. "I didn't need to."

I'm not sure if it's because Rax was here or what, but I got so swept up in the wild high, I didn't pay attention to myself. I enjoyed watching Shades getting off way too much.

And bossing him and Rax around sexually wasn't half bad, either. Jesus Christ.

Shades looks to Rax. "Help me out."

Rax swaggers over, still stroking himself. "Sure."

Shades lifts me by the armpits and shoves me into Rax's waiting arms. Rax supports me under the butt like a human chair, facing Shades, with my legs spread wide. I grin and lean into the rock star behind me to tease the rock star in front of me.

Rax braces himself against the brick wall. Now it's Shades's turn to get on his knees. Rax adjusts position so my cunt parallels Shades's mouth.

"Your pussy beads droplets like dew on flower blossoms." Shades flicks out his studded tongue and dips in for a quick drink.

"God, you're such a poet." I relax into Rax's arms. He stares down my front and watches with a shit-eating grin.

Shades strokes my tits under the shirt. He pulls on a nipple, pinches, tweaks.

"Tell him what you want, Letty," Rax whispers in my ear.

I don't tell him what I really want, which is two dicks in my twat. I'll save that for my next birthday. "Tongue-fuck me, Shades."

"Gladly." His deep voice vibrates my clit. He licks just inside my fat, swollen lips and makes slow, exaggerated sweeps up, down, left, right, in, out, coaxing those hot juices from deep inside my cunt.

"Now stick your fingers in." I caress his dark hair, taming the gel-hardened line down the middle. "Two of them."

He does. Then he laps up an escaping trickle while pumping me. He puts his palm into it, increasing the speed. His mouth retreats when he finds my happy spot, and I cry out. Rax's grip tightens. I'm trapped between two men I should hate.

My breath flies in and out in great gasps. My legs buck against the onslaught of rising ecstasy. My hips grind desperately against his driving fingers.

"God, please … please make me come, Shades." My body is on the verge of breaking apart. I'm coming undone, unraveling, seduced by my enemies, but dying for more. "Yes, yes, yes …"

Arching my back into Rax's front, I cut loose a spray of clear fluid all over Shades's arm. I twist, wrestle, and caterwaul as the climax consumes the last of my control in a quick burst.

Rax's triumphant laughter draws me back to reality. When I come to, Shades is grinning like the joker in a deck of cards, fingers still lodged inside me, covered in my squirt juice.

"What the fuck happened?" I can't catch my breath.

Rax lowers me to the ground. Shades holds me up because I seriously can't stand.

"Who fucking cares?" Rax zips up his jeans.

I tug my skirt over the natural disaster that was once my vagina and swipe my ass. Something sticky …

"Goddamn it, Rax." He must've come when I did. All over the back of my skirt.

He scurries away and blows a kiss. "That's for you to remember me by." And he's gone.

My head swims. I face Shades. I'm an awkward mess of rushing endorphins, would-be shame, and horrified realizations.

"Have we royally fucked up?" He probably thinks I'm talking about what happened with Rax, but I'm more worried about my change in feelings for *him*. This can't be good.

He grabs me by the soaking wet cooch, crooks a finger in, and pulls me to his side. "If we did, it was worth it." He kisses me stupid.

Strings

I think I've made a terrible mistake.
I think I'm falling for Shades.

I'D WEAR A DICK HAT ONSTAGE

The next day, I wake alone in my bunk to a *bumpity-bump* vibration. I should sleep with this shitty phone between my legs.

Text from Shades: *U need 2 register your pussy as a lethal weapon.*

I giggle and write back, *Why?*

My balls need a fucking sling this morning.

That bad? I type.

That good.

He's not the only one suffering. My lady garden and adjacent environs took a hell of a beating last night. But like Shades said, it was totally fucking worth it.

The emotional part gets buried until I've had a chance to process it properly. Can't deal with that shit right now, even though I kinda want to dance across the parking lot, singing tunes from *The Sound of Music*.

I can't believe we did it with Rax. Question is, will he keep quiet or blab to everyone and their donkey? He has nothing to lose by telling Kate what we got up to. It would probably make him pretty damn happy to be rid of her—and Jinx and me too. Less competition to worry about, that's for sure. And one less whiny bitch on his case all the time.

Yep, Rax is totally gonna spill. Hopefully it'll be later, rather than sooner. I should be upset or at least worried, but it's hard to care about much when you wake to a morning-after like this.

I yawn and stretch in my little bed. Shades and me. Engaged in hard-core anal behind the bus. With Rax. And squirts.

That's twice Shades has turned me into a human fire hose during sex. I should consider a career in porn.

I crawl out of bed and head for the bathroom. On the way, I overhear Jillian and Freddie talking.

"What do you mean the credit card's been declined?" she says.

"I tried it three times. Even went inside and had them run it there. It's no good," Freddie replies.

I stop to look out the window. We're parked at a gas station.

Jillian sighs loudly. "Let me talk to Todd." She storms down the aisle to his bunk and calls his name.

Shit. What's this about? I go into the toilet cubicle, do my business, and beeline to the front of the bus. Jillian, Freddie, and Shades are outside engaged in a lively discussion. Having been born with no shame or sense of privacy, I trudge down the steps in my holey flannel pajama pants and worn fuzzy slippers.

"What's going on?"

Jillian cracks me with a mind-your-own business frown. "Nothing. Go back inside."

I turn to Shades, drop my hands to my hips, and resist shivering despite the freezing temperature. "Nothing?"

He clenches his jaw. I can't read his expression behind those damned sunglasses. After a good fifteen seconds of silence, he says, "My credit card's been cut off."

I straighten. Well, ain't that the shit? The prince gets to see what it's like to live on the ass-end of the dollar sign like the rest of us lowlifes. This ought to be a riot. "Did you piss off your father?"

Now it's Shades's turn to smack me with a scowl. He faces Freddie. "How much is it? I've got some cash."

"Four hundred bucks."

My lids snap wide open. It costs *that* much to fill up a fucking bus?

Shades edges past me up the steps.

"What the hell is going on, Jillian?" I say as soon as he's out of earshot.

She drags me to the back wheels. "This is why I didn't want to say anything. I tried to minimize the potential for freak-outs, but you can't let shit go, can you?"

Jillian's clearly upset, but I need answers. "Come on, this is my tour too. I think we have a right to know what our money situation is."

Her eyes spark as if they're about to birth some poison darts in my general direction. "You want to know the truth? There *is* no money. Todd agreed to pay for all the travel expenses," she lowers her voice and tosses a glance to Freddie, "including our driver's salary and stocking the bus, and now his cash flow is dry. Our deal was if we made any money after everyone was paid, he'd get reimbursed. If not …"

"So, Shades has been funding this *whole* operation from the beginning?" Holy mother of God. "Why?"

Jillian's hard gaze softens. "Because he's like you, Letty. He wants to make it. He wants to prove to his dad and the rest of the world that he's a great musician."

If her words were knives, I'd be bleeding out from multiple stab wounds. My nose suddenly tingles, a warning of an imminent tear attack on the eyeballs.

Shades told me before he had something to prove, but I figured the high-horse "music is my passion" diatribe was just a thinly veiled cover for what he really wanted—booze, free poontang, and an express ticket out from under King Armstrong's thumb.

Shades paid for the driver, food, and gas. Wow.

I assumed he was like every other rich bitch I've met: full of himself, entitled, and better than everyone else.

But really, when has he ever exhibited any of those qualities? That kind of person sounds a lot more like—

Me.

And now my thoughts turn their pointy knives inward. *Et tu, Letty?*

Man, sometimes I can be so unaware. And unsympathetic.

What a fucking dickhead I am.

Shades comes out of the convenience store, hands in his pockets, head down. He slinks around the corner of the store. I sidestep so I can see him. Scowling, he runs his hands through his hair a couple times, takes several deep breaths, and looks at the bus like a forlorn puppy. He turns around and kicks the shit out of a discarded Coke can. Another frustrated finger-combing session turns into furious hair rubbing.

Shit. I feel bad for him. I want to jump into his arms, wrap myself around him in a full-body hug, and squeeze him for a day. But I can't, thanks to these strings that tie me to Kate and Jinx. Goddamn it, I wish I could make the rest of the world disappear for a few hours.

I look back to Jillian. "Okay, let me get this straight. We didn't make enough money from the nights we played to cover the fuel costs?"

"There's a little. None of the shows were sold out. I was planning to wait a week to pay everyone so you'd each get a bigger amount. Now it looks like we'll have to spend our profits on travel after all. Unless Todd or someone else has a secret stash in their underwear drawer."

"We need a plan before we hit Jacksonville."

Jillian nods grimly. "Time to get creative." She pushes me toward the door.

We climb aboard. Rax and Toombs share a couch. Both look hungover. I avoid Rax's eyes like they're contagious. Still can't believe I let that asshole fuck me. And go down on me. And come on the back of my skirt.

Jinx picks at a dent in her drumstick. Dark glasses in place, Shades mounts the steps and assumes a tough-guy pose, leaning against the divider between the lounges and bunks. My heart aches for him.

Kate stands away from everyone else, arms folded over her chest, and huffs. "What the fuck is going on, Jillian? There's no money? We aren't getting paid?"

Jillian holds up both hands. "Wait a minute. You *will* get paid, just not as much as I'd hoped. We've run into a snag with funding," she doesn't look at Shades, "but I think we can make up for it with some creative marketing."

"Fuck. I should've known this whole tour was a sham from the beginning. Way too good to be true." Kate turns and stomps down the aisle.

"Hold on, Kate," Jillian says. "I'm trying to solve a problem, and I need your help."

"Then ask your precious boys. I didn't sign on to solve your problems."

"They're *everyone's* problems." Jillian's voice turns icy. "If you don't want to be a team player, you're welcome to get off the bus any time."

The muscles in Kate's cheek ripple. "I'm starting to think that's a good idea."

"Please, Kate. Let's hear Jillian out." Jinx so rarely speaks—especially in emotionally charged situations like this—that I drop my jaw.

Toombs glances her way.

"Let her go." Rax doesn't look up from his slouch on the couch.

"Mind your own fucking business," I say. I'm walking a tightrope, but if Kate thinks everyone's ganging up on her, she'll totally walk. And if she walks, that's it for Cherry Buzz Float.

Rax scowls but shuts up.

"If you want someone to blame, it's me," Shades pipes in. "I committed to covering travel. As soon as I get the money, I'll pay everyone back."

He's gonna use his own cash—not his dad's—to pay *us* back? Man, I *totally* pegged him wrong. And my beaver's back to its old juicy tricks. Thanks a lot, Shades.

"You don't owe me anything," I say, knowing Kate won't like it. I may be poorer than dirt, but if there's one thing I've learned from Shades, it's how to appreciate what little I do have. Fuck, who needs money anyway?

Gulp.

He presses his lips together in a tight, fake smile.

"Me neither," Jinx adds in her sweet, quiet voice.

Kate narrows her eyes.

Rax waves a dismissive hand and looks away. "Fine. Me neither."

Toombs and Shades's gazes intersect. "We're square," Toombs says in his gruff voice.

Shades nods at us but doesn't say anything. It's gotta be a huge blow to his ego to go from King of the Hill one moment to starving sewer rat the next.

"See how easy things are when everyone plays nice?" Jillian shoots Kate a loaded glower. "Okay, here's the plan. If we want to make money, we need to sell out shows from now on. We've got a number of free tools at our disposal to do that: social networking, being more visible and talking to fans, and giveaways."

"Giveaways aren't free," Rax says. "At least not for the person giving shit away."

Jillian smiles. "Of course, they are. Ever since you mentioned the lap-dance video challenge, I've been brainstorming ideas. Since you guys are so fond of dares, why not give your fans what they really want?"

My stomach twists into a cherry stem knot. "Like…?"

"Something edgy. Seductive. Hot. And most of all, fun."

I raise a brow.

Jillian gestures around the bus. "You're good-looking people. Tell your fans every time you sell out a show, you'll perform in bikinis and Speedos."

"Hell no."

"Fuck that."

"Have you lost your fucking mind?"

"I'd wear a dick hat onstage."

All heads turn to Toombs. Did he really say that? I bust the fuck out laughing. In three seconds, everyone else is busting a gut too. Well, everyone except Kate, of course.

Once we settle down, Jillian says, "Get on your smartphones and put it out on your fan pages. Ask people to spread the word. We hit Jacksonville tonight. Two big shows means you have the potential to sell a fuckload of tickets. Make it happen." She pauses to glance at Kate. "Or not."

As the party breaks, they all drag out their phones— naturally, I look like a big twat because my damn phone only speaks Caveman—and start typing. Girls stay in front, and boys go to the back. I sigh as Shades walks away. The glasses over his eyes don't hide his furrowed brow. Poor guy must be humiliated.

Fuck that whole "no strings attached" rule.

I shake my head and face my bandmates. "We've got a few hours before we get to Florida. Practice?"

Kate scowls like she burned her tongue on the bitter pile of hot, steaming shit Jillian forced her to swallow. "Whatever." She grabs her guitar and headphones.

The three of us tune in to Kate's portable and play.

New melodies wind their way through the old ones in my head. Notes and lyrics float around me. All of them connect to Shades. He's taken hold of my heartstrings and won't let go. It's a scary feeling. I've been in love a few times. At least I thought it was love. This is different.

At first, it was all about the sex. Now it's not. That's the part that scares me.

A screaming guitar interrupts my thoughts and the

song. Frowning, I yank off my headphones. "What the fuck?"

Rax sits at the opposite end of the bus, guitar in hands, wailing on the beast at full volume through a portable speaker. Beside him, Toombs leans over a Fender Stratocaster I've never seen before and screeches out a harmony that perfectly complements Rax's lead.

Since when does Toombs play guitar? I glance over at Jinx, whose mouth hangs open as she blatantly stares at him.

Shades joins them on bass, the credit card incident apparently forgotten.

If Kate weren't here, I'd be in total awe watching the three of them—especially Toombs. He's good. *Really* fucking good.

"You mind turning it down a little?" I yell to placate Kate. Her complexion is three shades darker than normal, and the muscles in her cheeks ripple like an oncoming storm.

No one in Killer Dixon can hear me. I can't hear myself.

So, I rummage around under the couch until I find my little monitor. I plug in, turn the thing up to full volume, and join in the guys' song. The deep vibrations rock the bus, travel through every solid surface. I aim the head of my bass at them like a gun and imagine the tuning pegs are bullets.

Blam, blam, blam!

Oh yeah, motherfuckers. Take that.

I stalk down the tight aisle toward Killer Dixon, slapping my strings in answer to their musical summons like a cat in heat, looking for some action. All three men smile at me heading their way.

Rax offers a seductive melody.

I reciprocate with a supporting line.

Shades tosses out a series of complicated runs on his

bass.

I lick my lips and answer with a similar but more evolved ruckus.

Toombs backs up Rax with an on-the-go rhythm and watches with detached interest.

Sonic booms duel between Shades and me, and Rax is caught in the middle. Kinda reminds me of last night.

In three more seconds, it's a balls-out jam session of improvisation, rocking new strains, and bold calls and responses.

I blend into that magic, fall into the arms of the music, and let it cover me. Time and space disappear. Flow consumes me. I lose track of my body, and my fingers take me where they want to go.

They lead me to Shades. Always back to Shades.

I open my eyes—when did I close them?—and he's in front of me. The necks of our basses almost touch, our strings only inches apart.

Just like the invisible ones drawing us closer and closer each passing day.

How did this happen? How did I get so lost in him?

My fingers dance over the frets as I pluck, and suddenly my music—and the magic—crashes to a deafening halt.

I pause. Turn around. Kate holds up my unplugged cord and slams it on the floor. She stomps to her bunk and slashes the curtain shut. The guys stop playing, and the spell breaks. Along with my heart.

Shit. Caught naked again, and not in the good way. Avoiding male gazes, I blink away the gathering tears and return to Jinx with my head lowered.

She hugs me and whispers into my hair, "That was awesome, Letty."

"Thanks." I stow my bass. Can't do this anymore. On the way to my bunk, I sneak a peek at Jillian. She has a tear in her eye too.

WOMANBALLS IN BIKINIS

After hiding in my bedicle—a new word I invented for my bed/cubicle—and listening to Killer Dixon practicing all day, I venture out to see where we are. The bus is parked behind tonight's venue. And holy fuck, this place is huge.

"Letty," Jillian says. "Glad you could join us."

Back to being her usual hard-ass self so soon? I shouldn't be surprised. I'll bet her uterus is made of rusted iron.

I glance around. It's just her. Jinx and Kate are talking in back. "Where's everyone else?"

"I sent them to the grocery. Since we're cutting expenses, we're gonna have to stop eating fast food and start cooking."

I laugh. "You sent a bunch of *guys* grocery shopping? You didn't give them any money, did you? They'll just come back with beer and call it a protein substitute."

Jillian shakes her head. "They have a list. I was very direct with my instructions."

I shrug. "Okay."

"Looks like our social network strategy is working," Jillian continues. "The event organizer tells me they're fifty tickets shy of selling out tonight, and about a hundred away for tomorrow."

"And that means ...?"

"You're on standby for bikini detail."

"Well, good thing I don't have one."

Jillian grins. "I told the boys if they brought back everything on my grocery list, they could go shopping at the surf shop."

"There aren't any surf shops in Jacksonville." Shit, at least I hope there aren't.

"There's one right around the corner."

"How is *that* fair? *They* get to pick out *our* bathing suits?" Not that I mind Shades seeing me in one, but hundreds of fans?

Actually ...

I smile. This could be fun.

"Okay, fine. Bikini. Whatever. What are the guys wearing tonight?"

Jillian arches a brow. "What would you *like* for them to wear?"

I toss out a laugh. "Well ... since we're on a tight budget, we can't spend much. Is there a thrift store nearby?"

"I like where this is going," Jillian says with a wicked grin.

Me too.

I grab Jinx (of course, Kate refuses to have anything to do with our plan), and the three of us walk a couple of blocks to the thrift store for supplies. A hundred bucks—thank Jesus for Jillian's generous credit card donation—and two hours later, we return to the bus with huge smiles.

"It's about time you got back," Rax says. "Kate's so excited to see what we bought you, she's been masturbating in her bed all day."

"Fuck you, dickhole." Kate's shrill scream billows her bunk curtain.

Jinx cringes.

Wow, screechy-stabby much? I'm starting to wonder about Kate's mental state. She seems to unravel a little more every day. I make a note to sneak through her shit later to be sure she doesn't have any weapons hidden in her trundle.

I drop my bags to the floor and hitch my hands to my hips. "Do your worst." Bad choice of words, I'm sure, but I gotta at least pretend to have some womanballs about this.

Shades and Toombs gather behind Rax as he unveils his purchases. Shades winks at me.

Oh boy.

"This, my *juicy* little Letty, is yours."

I wince at the reference to last night. *Nice, cocksucker.*

Rax pulls out a red, white, and blue starred-and-striped two-piece thong bikini. Without looking at the size on the tag, I'm certain it's for a ten-year-old. A really slutty one.

With one finger so as not to attract too many germs from the surely diseased thing, I hook the stringed whore-wear and dangle it before my eyes. "This is the most disgusting piece of shit I've ever seen."

Rax nods eagerly. "I know, right?" He whips out a color-coordinated pom pom on a stick and shakes it into my other hand. "For your bass."

I tilt my head and let out a long breath. It's just for tonight. Okay, maybe tomorrow night too.

"I guess this means I gotta annihilate my bushes." I glance down. "Fuck you very much, Rax."

"My pleasure, little squirt." He ruffles my hair.

I slap his hand away. Motherfucker. That's okay. My comeuppance is on its way.

Shades turns his head as if to hide the smile I already saw. Oh, he's getting his too.

Kate rolls out of bed and approaches with fists balled under her arms.

Rax turns to Jinx. "And for you, wildcat ..." He holds up a leopard print monokini and a matching pair of cat ears.

Oh Christ.

Jinx flips Toombs a pointed stare, accepts the flimsy fabric, and says, "Thanks." She wanders to her bunk, keeping her gaze locked on Toombs until she gets there. Jinx the Minx. Damn, girl.

The dude cracks a smile—like, a genuine one. I think it might be his first time. Jinx popped Toombs's smile cherry!

"And finally, for our lovely princess, Kate ..." Rax unveils a frou-frou, cotton candy-looking piece of nastiness made out of those super soft feathers. I assume it's a two-piece, but I can't tell for all the allergy-inducing fluffery. "I know how much she loves pink."

I purse my lips. Wow.

Out of nowhere, Kate storms to Rax, snatches the outfit, and stuffs it in his laughing mouth. "You fucking wear it, ball bag!"

"Whoa!" I grab her from behind and try to drag her away, but the banshee snarls and claws and howls like a rabid squirrel on crack. What the fuck got into her?

Shades and Toombs grapple with Rax, who's now equally enraged. Fire burns hot in his face.

Jillian rushes toward us, waving her hands. "Everybody chill the hell out!"

Kate elbows me in the ribs—great, some bruises to show off with my new get-up—and kicks at Rax. His bandmates on either side, holding him back, Rax huffs and puffs like he's ready to blow the bus down.

Jillian gets up in Kate's personal space and points a quivering finger in her face. "Bitch, I've just about had it with you." Her voice is low and even. "This is your last chance to pull your shit together. One more outburst, and either you walk, or I do. I don't get paid enough to babysit your immature ass. What's it gonna be?"

I've never seen Jillian so angry. Her expression flaunts crazed intensity that rivals Kate's. She's reached the red zone on her Kate-o-meter.

I step between them. "Kate, if you don't want to wear the outfit, don't. It's not that big of a deal."

"I'm *not* putting that shit on." Her words come out more like a hollow growl than a recognizable sentence.

Laying my hands on her heaving shoulders, I say, "Calm down, okay? It was just a joke." Now I'm seriously worried for her mental state. Kate's a wounded animal, and Rax is the one who hurt her. Repeatedly.

"Come on. Let's get some air." I lead her toward the steps.

Once we're outside, she says, "That fucker is doing everything he can to provoke me."

"You're right. He is. But you don't have to let him get under your skin. Look at yourself. You nearly instigated a riot in there. Rax may be a douche grenade, but I don't think he'd ever hurt you. You gotta pull yourself together and give up this grudge. Dwelling on it is making you psycho."

"*I'm* psycho?" She jabs an index finger into her chest. "He stole my song, Letty. How would you feel if he'd done that to you? Music is my *life*. He's trying to deprive me of my happiness." Tears fill her bloodshot eyes.

With a tentative hand, I smooth her hair and hug her. "Music isn't everything," I say into her neck.

She pulls away. "It is to me."

I want to comfort her. To say the right words that'll make her see how crazy she sounds, but she's too far gone at this moment to understand. "Okay, Kate. Let's not argue anymore. We have a show to get ready for. Wear a pair of jeans and a T-shirt if you'd rather. No pressure."

She sets her jaw and nods. I return to the bus, pick up my dropped bags from the thrift store, and hand them half-heartedly to each of the guys. When I get to Shades, I flash him a weak smile. He brushes my hand. I need to talk to him. Alone.

I look through the window at Kate pacing furiously across the blacktop, and I feel the strings between her and me loosen as the ones binding me to Shades tighten.

135

I have a bad feeling the tension is heading for a snap.

* * * *

"Yo, yo, yo! Jacksonville!" I holler into the mic before a packed house. Holy mother of Cthulu, this is the biggest gig I've ever played. Two thousand people. It's a good thing I don't get stage fright. "How are y'all motherfuckers doin' this fine December night?"

Screams, stomping feet, and whistles answer.

"We're Cherry Buzz Float, and we're here to blow your minds, light a fire under your asses, and take you back to a time when the women knew how to rock just as hard as the men. You know what I'm talking about?"

Shouts and cheers.

"I'm talking about the magical '70s." I shrug out of my jacket to reveal the way-too-small bikini top with big white stars over my nipples.

The crowd roars, and I gotta admit, I'm a little wet in the thonger that they seem to like what they see. Such an attention whore I am.

"Now, who wants to get musically fucked by three chicks armed with sexually charged instruments of mass distraction?"

Pandemonium.

Lady gusher.

"Let's go!" I scream with my best Janis Joplin voice and kick into "Take It Like a Man."

As I sing and slap my strings, I embrace the warmth of the fans surrounding me. The music takes control, and off I go, into my zone. The stage buffs away the scars from the earlier drama.

Tonight as I play, I feel Shades with me. When I glance to the side stage, he's there, watching, smiling, and clapping with the fans.

I want to make music and happy endings with Shades.

Just like this. Jamming with him and the guys on the bus was amazing and fresh and new. I want to live that feeling every day of my life. That oneness with the dude I care about.

Yeah, I do care about him. A lot more than I should.

As I hit my favorite bass groove, I shoot him a saucy grin, and he returns it. God, I so wanna do him after this show. But even more, I want to talk to him. I want to *know* him.

The crowd vibrates with contagious energy. At the end of the first tune, I grow a pair of balls and go all out.

"Thank you, guys. Whoa, is it hot in here, or what?" I fan myself and lift my skirt, flapping nice and slow. The guys at my feet go nuts. I face Jinx, who casually undoes her sensible white button-down and tosses the shirt aside, revealing her leopard print monokini. She looks hot as hell, like she's ready to rip out the throats of every guy in the place after she has her way with them. Wow. Maybe Jinx is coming out of her shell.

I drop a pick and bend over to get it, baring my thronged little ass to God and everybody and shimmying slowly back to a vertical position. The whistles become deafening. Jinx smiles at me. Mutual respect passes between us. Damn, I love that chick.

Wearing a trench coat with his hair slicked back, Shades watches from the sidelines, arms folded over his chest, brow raised, grinning from ear to ear. Rax and Toombs flank him with similar expressions. Jillian gives us a thumbs-up.

Meanwhile, Kate stands to the side in her ripped jeans and T-shirt, studying her fingernails. Whatever.

"Let's rock!" I shout into the mic. The music kicks. I shake, sing, and scream. The crowd roars. The world disappears.

At the end of our set, I tell the fans, "If you wanna see more of us," I heft my star-spangled boobs, "go give our fan page a like. I made a deal with Killer Dixon that if we get more fans than they have, I'll take off the skirt at tomorrow night's show."

The guys in the front lift their beers up high. "Yeah, baby! Fuck, yeah!"

I prance off stage behind Kate and Jinx like I own the fucking universe. I brush Shades's chest as I leave, and he swipes the back of my thigh.

"Lookin' good," he mumbles.

"Thanks for the duds," I say as I mosey past him. "Can't wait to see yours." It sucks that I can't kiss him or at least grab his ass.

He, Rax, and Toombs gawk as we greet a few fans backstage. Kate signs some autographs, then disappears while the crew help Jinx break down her kit. Typical of the selfish bitch to leave Jinx hanging. Fine. I start to join Jinx, but Jillian grabs my arm.

"You sold out," she says. "Both shows."

"Rock on."

"Not bad, Letty." She pats my shoulder and smiles.

"What can I say? Tits and ass sell."

"We both know that's only part of it. Your fans are here for the music."

"Is there anything else?" I laugh and head over to help with the drums, intentionally flashing the crowd here and there. It's fun to get a rise out of the guys.

When Killer Dixon hits the stage, the noise level jumps again, and it's my turn to stalk Shades.

The boys walk out wearing long trench coats and stop in the center of the platform. At once they don ugly-ass glasses with tape on the bridges of the noses, snap open their coats like strippers, and toss them to the floor.

Shades has on plaid pants pulled halfway up his chest that flood so badly, they show off at least three inches of his red and black argyle socks and holey black loafers. Wide brown suspenders keep his short-sleeved button-down shirt—complete with pens in pocket—under wraps. Tattoos down his forearms totally ruin the outfit in the best way possible. But the bright red bow tie? Fucking priceless.

Rax and Toombs are dressed similarly with clashing colors. The geek squad has arrived.

Oh my God, I nearly shit myself laughing.

Kate appears at my side, scowling as usual. How can she not find the humor in this scene?

Shades slings his bass strap across his shoulder and grabs the mic. "How about Cherry Buzz Float, huh? They make me wanna stick my dick in a wall socket." He makes an exaggerated adjustment in the crotch area. I smile.

The fans cheer. I would too, if Kate weren't around.

Glancing our way, Rax says into his mic, "I only wish we coulda seen what Kate had going on under those jeans. I'll bet that pussy can get a cat purring, no?"

Oh shit. What's that asshole doing? Besides making my life hell?

Kate's nostrils flare, and her lips press together tightly. She stomps off in a fury as Killer Dixon launches into their first song. Great. Fucking great.

I stay side stage for the entire set because: 1) I'm not interested in running damage control when Kate loses her shit; and 2) I can't resist watching Shades. The guy has a gorgeous, rough voice that gives me cooter quivers. And the way he moves—so casual. He's the physical embodiment of a living, breathing swagger. Even in his ridiculous outfit, looking like a total fucking imbecile, I want to do him all night long. He's proof that clothes do not make the man. His music does.

And just as he knows how to work me from top to bottom, he works his crowd like a pro. He senses the highs and the lulls and improvises to give the fans what they crave. He's pure rock star. Pure perfection.

I know I promised myself not to get attached, but I've

changed my mind about him.

I want him all over me, every minute, twenty-four/seven. I want to be tied up in his strings forever and a day. I want Todd Armstrong.

PISSING DUDES AND ROGUE EJACULATORS

The guys insist on hitting the strip club after the show. Rax knows the owner, so they get in free. I'll bet they get free drinks all night too.

Cherry Buzz Float isn't invited.

I'm pouty. I could use some liquor, and I want to know what's going on inside. I don't like the thought of strippers—or anyone else—touching Shades. Since crashing Killer Dixon's party isn't an option, I'm outside with Jinx and Jillian in the freezing cold, still wearing my too-short skirt, flirting with guys as they go in.

At least I'm getting some work done.

Jillian got the brilliant idea to have some cheap cards printed up with info about Cherry Buzz Float and links to our website and fan page. I know she did this as a special favor, so I'm showing my appreciation by playing the cool rock chick and making nice with the locals. But my attention keeps wandering to that imposing door. Maybe Shades will come up with an excuse to go back to the bus early, and I'll have him to myself for a few minutes.

But the night wears on. No sign of him. After an hour of chatting with guys in the cold and giving away all our swag, Jillian has had it.

"I'm going in to get them," she declares, her breath mingling with wisps of cigarette smoke rising from her hand. "It's almost 1 a.m."

Perfect opportunity for me to jump in. "I'll go. I have to pee anyway."

"Fine. But if you're not back in five minutes, we're leaving. The parking lot is about to close, and we have to move the bus."

"I gotta pee too," Jinx says.

Jillian rolls her eyes. "Make it snappy."

·I high-five Jinx, and we break for the door. The bouncer has been talking to us all night, and he lets us in without paying cover. Thank God.

The place is dark, and the music's loud. I sift through the haze until a familiar, loud voice catches my attention. Rax. Drunk. And singing.

The members of Killer Dixon are parked in a rounded leather banquette in the sectioned-off VIP area at the back of the joint. Six strippers surround them. Jinx and I walk over.

Make that seven strippers. One of them is in Shades's lap with his arm around her hip. His hand rests on her naked thigh.

I inhale a deep breath to calm a sudden bout of rage-induced hypothermia.

A raven-haired beauty twirls her way down their personal pole to the tune of Rax singing, "Lo-lo-lo-la-Lola, you got my cock so swole-ah ... You swing on your pole-ah ... Can I shove my meat in your hidey-hole-ah?" He cracks himself up laughing and tips over onto Toombs's shoulder. The gyrating stripper smiles as she makes her way to him. He lifts his head and stares like an acid tripper enthralled by a fucking disco ball.

Waiting to be noticed, I lay my hands on my hips and try to be cool. When no one looks at me, I say, "Jillian says it's time to roll, guys."

Shades's head snaps up, but I can't read his expression. Damn sunglasses. I stare at him for several seconds.

Why am I so pissed about him being with another chick? Because this growing attraction makes me vulnerable. I'm not a fan of weakness.

I freak. I can't take seeing him with someone else. I bolt and leave Jinx standing there alone.

"Piss break," Rax says behind me.

Fuck. I gotta get to the bus. I don't want to be jealous, but I can't help my feelings. I've never been possessive about guys before. It's not me. I'm a free-spirit. A go-with-the-flow girl. A kite sailing on the breeze—

"Hey." A hand lands on my arm and stops me. Rax. Shit, I so don't want to deal with him right now.

I toss his hand off and face him. "What? And don't say you want to do it again. That was a one-time thing, man."

He herds me to the wall with his body but doesn't touch.

I lean in as if to kiss him. "If you tell anyone what happened, I'll rip your balls off with my teeth and spit them up your asshole."

"I won't tell if you don't. Our little secret." His words are sloppy slurs. Alcohol pours off his breath and slaps me in the face. Goddamn tease.

Secret? I thought for sure he was going to spill—

Understanding flares a series of connections in my brain, and equations add up. Rax's motivation is no longer an enigma. I dish a lopsided grin. "You don't want Toombs to find out about us."

His dull eyes flash for a split second. In his drunken state, he probably didn't mean to give up that little tidbit of info, but I'm so glad he did.

"You and Toombs have some kinda bromance thing brewing between you, and you don't want your lover boy to get jealous." I poke his chest.

The fact that he doesn't deny my accusation proves I'm right.

He inches in, and now we're so close, we might as well kiss and get it over with. Except kissing isn't on the agenda. I have no more interest in Rax than he has in me.

Yeah, this closeness is testosterone-driven, all right, but protectiveness is number one on the agenda, not sex.

"Toombs doesn't do well with being left out," he

mumbles, lids drooping to half-mast.

"I see. Take my advice and stay away from me and Jinx. And stop antagonizing Kate. No more repeats of your antics onstage tonight."

"Kate's a fucking bitch and deserves whatever she gets. She stole that song from *me*, not the other way around." His volume and wildly flailing arms draw attention from a couple walking by.

I conjure my best Cheshire cat smile and pat his cheek. "If clinging to lies gets you through the day, you keep on believing them. But the next time you get Kate worked up, I'm gonna seriously consider investing in a truth-dishing session with your lover Toombs."

"He's not my lover."

I don't believe him. "No? What do *you* call it, then?"

"He's my tag-team buddy." He awkwardly tweaks my nipple.

I bat his hand away. "Well, your *buddy* has eyes for Jinx, and that shit needs to stop."

He leans back with a loose, brain-addled grin. "Jinx is a big girl. Or at least, she will be when Toombs and I finish with her."

Nobody messes with Jinx while I'm around. I grab him by the nuts and drag him back within kissing distance. "I strongly urge you to reconsider," I whisper against his mouth.

His lips part, and for a second, I'm sure he's diving in. But he doesn't. "Looks like we got us a stalemate, Squirt."

"Indeed, we do." We visually throw down in silence for ten solid seconds before he backs off and stumbles toward the table, arms swinging and feet tripping.

Fucking asshole. I trudge in the direction of the door, but a leather blockade stops my paces. Shades. He grabs my wrist, ushers me around the corner, and pushes me against the wall with his lips.

I promptly dissolve into the wood.

Wait a minute. I'm supposed to be mad at him for flirting with other women. I reach up to shove him away, but my traitorous hands wind around his shoulders instead. The metal nub in his tongue tickles me. I caress it, and a flood of cooch juice pours out the freshly opened dam. I swear I'm gonna start believing in that pheromone shit. Every time this guy comes around, my pussy leaks. Lucky for me, he's the worst plumber in town.

He interrupts the delicious kissing with mumbles into my lips. "Stay away from Rax."

"Fuck you," I mumble back. Normally I'd resent a man telling me what to do, especially where other guys are concerned, but Shades's apparent jealousy trips my pride trigger. "I'll do whatever the fuck I want with Rax. Just like you do with your strippers."

He pulls away and nails me with a stare. "Strippers bore me."

"Yeah? You didn't look very bored at the table."

"Are you jealous?"

"Not at all," I lie.

He shoots a glance left, then right. He presses his cock against my hip. "Well, I am. And if I see you alone with Rax again, I'm gonna beat the living hell out of him. You don't want me to resort to violence, do you?" His rugged voice gets my uterus on her feet and dancing, but his words circulate warmth through my heart.

"Don't tell me who I can or can't be with." Evil twin Letty speaks with my mouth. I sure as shit wasn't thinking those words. Quite the opposite.

He dips closer and brushes my mouth with his. "How about if I ask real nice?"

"How about you give me a reason not to be with Rax? Or anybody else, for that matter."

The rich rock-star Lothario bullshit drops with a thud, and an air of truth fills the empty space between us. He pins me with those gorgeous emerald eyes. "I dig you,

Letty."

Shit, he did *not* just say that. I release a long breath, lay my palms on his chest, and drop the pretense too. Twenty million questions demand his immediate attention, and I ask the only one I shouldn't. "What the hell are we doing here? I mean, we had crazy-kinky sex that first night, and I swore to forget you. Then you show up with your fancy tour bus and money, and we're forced back together. We had butt sex on your birthday, but only because I promised. And then we did that shit with Rax. And now, here I am watching you fondle strippers and wondering what exactly *are* we?

"Shit, Shades. I'm no good with words in real-life situations. I write songs, not dialogue. I gotta know where I stand with you. This rubber ball bouncing inside my head is doing me in. Are we on, or are we off?"

I hope I didn't blow it by going full-on Letty, but this is who I am. What you see is what you get. If he doesn't like it, I'll walk away and deal. But walking away is gonna leave some nasty blisters on both my soles and my soul.

His curled finger and thumb pull my chin up, and the sincerity in his face incites my twat into mass production of rainbow cum bullets. I've got one in the chamber, and at least a couple more waiting anxiously in the magazine. *Ready, aim, fire!*

"You're the fucking craziest chick I've ever met, Letty. I wish all it took was a stripper and a lap dance to get you out of my head."

The block of ice entombing us cracks and crashes to the ground. I feel ten pounds lighter.

"Yeah? Well, it's hard to forget the woman who busted your ass cherry."

"Even that was ..." He shakes his head.

"You didn't like it." Ah, well, he's a good actor, I guess.

His face gets all serious. "I wouldn't have liked it with

anyone else."

Gush. "So, you *did* like it? Just a little?"

He holds up his thumb and index finger pinched within a half an inch of each other. "Maybe this much."

"Shit, are we, like, *talking* here?" Laughing, I gesture back and forth between us. "Because, I gotta say, the fucking is amazing, but having an actual conversation with you is out of this world."

He laughs too. "And here I was, contemplating another anal jam session with you. My timing's awful."

"Can't get enough of me, huh?"

He targets me with his heat-seeking gaze. The playfulness simmers away, leaving behind crystallized lust. "I can't."

This man totally does it for me. I lean in and kiss him, taking the care to do it right this time. His leather-jacketed arms enclose me, and my insides jiggle with adolescent glee. Last time I felt this warm was—

Never. That's right. Lusty heat usually rides on the back of the afterglow from great but casual sex. It emanates from down low, inside my naughty bits. It's primal and awesome, but short-lived.

The kind of heat I feel now is up higher. It's the rush of flapping wings in my gut. The quickening pulse in my neck. The flood of bliss in my heart. It radiates outward and doesn't stop.

This warmth—Shades's warmth—is like The Rock's.

I pull away. Shit. Have I found my other half?

"I don't like seeing you with strippers," I blurt out.

He doesn't miss a beat. "I don't like seeing you with Rax."

"Last night was—"

"—Hotter than solar flares in July, but ..." He pauses, licks his lips, then meets my gaze. God, how he unnerves me. "Let's not do it again."

I nod. "Okay."

I'm not sure, but I think we just made some kind of commitment. The flapping in my belly turns into full-blown birdie breakdancing. I lay a hand on my stomach. Doesn't settle anything, and I'm sorta glad. I like this squishy, flailing feeling.

A Lords of Acid song bites into the speakers, and everyone in the club runs for the center stage where some famous cover girl is doing her thing.

A slow smile spreads across Shades's beautiful face. God, the stud in the brow is kind of hot when he arches it like that. He glances over to the occupied crowd. "You wanna get down?"

"For fuck's sake, I thought you'd never ask." I giggle. "Where to, my rock prince?"

He takes my hand and leads me twenty feet to the bathroom. A few dudes stand around the urinals, but no one looks twice as Shades drags me by the skirt waistband into a handicap stall and slams the door shut.

I unhook his belt, unzip his jeans—thank God he changed out of those hideous stage clothes—and stroke his ready and willing todger. Low, staccato bass notes rattle the walls. Maybe the music will be loud enough to cover my gasps and moans. I plan to do a lot of that in here.

Before I can get on my knees to bow before the altar of Shades's glorious wanger and praise it with my mouth, he hefts me to the steel handle running parallel to the floor. It's not nearly deep enough to support me, so I drop a foot to the toilet seat and use that to help me balance on the bar. He lifts my skirt like a bride's veil and goes down on my screaming pussy, wiggling that goddamn tongue stud like a mini vibrator on my nub.

I comb my fingers through his sweat-dried hair, loving the feel of its softness mixed with the hard tugs on my clit. He sucks me loudly, hungrily. Thanks to my precarious position, I can barely move, which may have been his intention all along.

He makes out with my pussy. So fucking erotic. I'm about to blow after only two minutes of tongue tickling.

"I don't want to come yet, Shades. Not until you fill me with your cock." Even as I whisper the words, I push his mouth hard against my wet cunt and try again to thrust my stationary hips, to no avail.

He gets me up the mountain, and I put my foot down. I drag that beautiful fucking head to mine. I lick myself off his mouth, nice and slow so he can watch me and think about it. He parts his lips enough for me to lap the insides too. I stare into his eyes. "Mmm, I taste good on your mouth. I wonder how I taste on your cock."

"I dreamed of eating your pussy last night. Fucking devoured you."

God, he says the sweetest things!

"I've never had a man make me come like you do. Even with Rax involved, that was all you, baby."

I fondle his stiffy and use it to sop up a hearty helping of Letty's all-natural lube from my flooded muff. I spread the batter over the head of his cock with a thumb and chase it with my lips. I groan around my mouthful, savoring the delicacy. After only a minute of playtime, he takes my prize away and squeezes it. His tight expression is adorable when he concentrates. I resist the urge to pinch his cheeks.

I resume my position on the bar, spread my legs as wide as they'll go in this cramped space, and welcome General Shades to the safe haven of my eager love bunker. He slips in like an oiled eel and drives in and out, slow and steady.

God, I've found heaven. His name is Todd Armstrong.

My arms snake around his neck, and I tilt my head to enjoy the view as bliss diffuses through his face. In this nasty-ass strip club bathroom full of pissing dudes and possible rogue ejaculators, Shades is no longer some guy I love fucking. He's some guy I fucking love.

I stare at him too long, smiling like a doofus.

That's right. I can admit it now. I'm in love. Just a little. But enough.

His head drops to my shoulder.

"Making music with you on the bus was amazing." I lick the edge of his ear where a plug stretches his lobe. I shouldn't have said that, but I'm so raw and full of this crazy *need* to share my heart with him, I can't help it.

He lifts his head and caresses my cheek. "I wish things could be different." He's a little breathless. Just how I like him.

"Me too."

His slowing thrusts match my mood.

"I need to know one thing before you come all over my pussy."

Smiling, he says, "Better make it quick. I'm about to go Mt. St. Helens."

"When we met, you said you had no idea who I was."

"I didn't." He clamps a palm to my jaw and traces the line of my lower lip with his bedazzled tongue. Goddamn it, he makes it hard to concentrate.

"How did you know we'd see each other again after that first night? You made me promise to return the favor on your birthday."

"I told you. I'm lucky." The metal walls of the stall clank a solid, steady beat as he fucks me. "I knew fate would bring us back together at the right moment. Always happens like that for me. I trust in the power of the universe."

Tuned into the clanging beats, my mind hooks a rolling bass groove as it floats past.

"So that means everything will work out for us in the end." My words fall in line with the rhythm. "Whatever we … are?"

"Right on." He leans in and kisses me like he's got it all

150

figured out.

I wish I could trust like that.

Trust The Rock. It won't steer you wrong.

Yeah. True. I close my lids, absorb Shades's in-and-out flow, and visualize the notes playing in my brain. In the heat of this mad, passionate rush, I lose track of the bass line, and words transpose over the music, blurring and fading it ...

> *Pull my strings*
> *Make me sing*
> *Tie me in knots*
> *You're all I've got*
> *No matter what I do, I'm stuck with you*
> *Bound to your heart by these unbreakable strings*
> *When I'm with you, my soul has wings*

"Hell's bells, pussycat." He pulls out and slaps the head of his cock on my cunt. I swear I hear splashes. Or maybe that's just a guy shitting in the stall next door. "Where do you want it?"

"Right here." Maintaining my unstable balance between the toilet seat and the bar, I spread my pussy open with two fingers and tilt my hips up so he can see his pretty pink target.

Eyes glazed, he pumps his dick, and a surge of wet heat splatters my front door. Dear God, he's beautiful when he comes. His smile does me in. Hands down, Shades is the hottest thing in my universe.

Using his cum as lube, I finger fuck myself to orgasm, staring into those hypnotic green gems of his. In the moment when I tip over the edge, I want him to see in me what I saw in him—the things I can't say with words: devotion, adoration, and the Grand Poobah of them all, love.

His grin tells me the message got through loud and

clear.

I laugh and suck our combined juices off my fingers, scraping them with my teeth. He goes on one knee, steals a few quiet slurps of his own off my quivering twat, and then brings his wet lips and tongue to mine.

Fuck. Me.

We're absolutely to die for. A little salty, a little sour, but five stars any way you mix us.

I dissolve into his arms, his mouth, his everything. My head spins like a whirligig. With soft pulls, gentle sucks, playful swipes, he drags me into his light, his music. His Rock.

My body has always been a loud talker, just like my mouth, but right now, something else speaks on my behalf. I don't know if it's my heart, my soul, or both, but goddamn it, Shades has unearthed the music that makes me who I am and dragged it to the surface for inspection.

And I really like the way he inspects me. The seal of approval is evident in his tender kiss.

I want to tell him I love him. I want to scream it to the whole fucking world.

I stroke his rough cheek instead.

Someone bangs on the door. "Hey, how long you gonna be in there? I gotta drop a deuce real bad."

"Way to kill a moment, Dickie McDoucherson." I wave my middle finger over the top of the stall.

"Hey, somebody's banging a chick in there," a voice says. Laughter follows.

This is my life.

Shades stuffs his machinery back into its shed and zips up as I look on longingly.

I want more than this. I want cuddling and postcoital binge eating and spooning. I want to wake up beside him tomorrow morning and start all over again.

Fuck screwing in bathroom stalls and behind the tour bus. I want to share a bed with him. A real bed in a real house with real, clean sheets. I'm tired of sneaking around.

The main door opens. Loud music seeps in. "Letty, you in here?"

Oh, for shit's sake. It's Kate.

The guys on the other side snicker. "I don't know what her name is, but someone's getting stuffed in there."

Taps on the metal. Goddamn it, they're peeking through the cracks.

Shades puts his back to the door and holds me in front of him. "Fuck off," he calls.

"That you, Shades?" Kate says. She's close.

Fuck!

"Do you mind?" he replies with a double shot of agitation in his tone.

"Hurry up, asshole," she huffs. "It's bedtime."

The main bathroom door opens and closes a couple more times.

We wait a full minute before moving. I think I've been holding my breath at least that long.

"You go out first. Make sure the coast is clear," I whisper. "I'll come out in a bit. Do whatever you have to do to get Kate away from here."

He nods, pecks the soft spot behind my ear, and replies, "One day I'm gonna fuck you proper, foxy lady. See you on the bus."

I smile. Anyone else talking that '70s bullshit would sound like a total fucking head case, but it works for Shades. Fuck knows it works for me too.

He lays a panty-wringer of a kiss on me and struts out of the stall, smoothing his fauxhawk. The slaps of palms bounce off mirrors and tile, and roars of appreciative laughter barrel between the guys out there.

"Hey, you're the singer for Killer Dixon," one of the dudes says.

Oh, fuck-a duck-a.

"I'll bet you got a hot piece of ass, huh? Come on out, jailbait."

"Yeah, Killer Dixon. You wanna meet the band?" Shades says.

"They're here? Hell yeah, man."

The voices trail off, and the door closes again. I wait a few minutes. More people come in and go out. When it's mostly quiet, I sneak to the door, look both ways, and get the hell out of Dodge.

When I return to the guys' table, Shades is nowhere in sight, but Rax is sweet-talking the brunette from before. He's totally fucking wasted, pawing all over the poor girl who seems to be held against her will on his lap. His words slur so badly, they're almost indecipherable.

"See, Lola, that's why I want you to come to my big bus. I got all kindsa shit to show you there. Have you seen my bald-headed yogurt slinger?" He reaches for his belt buckle, but she lays a hand on his to stop him. "It's good to the last drop and built for speed. Strippers like big dicks, right?"

Nice. Could this asshole be any more insulting? Actually, yes, he probably could.

"Come on, man." Toombs pats him on the shoulder. "We gotta roll."

"But Lola and I were just getting to know each other." He reaches for the remains of his drink. I snatch and shoot it before he can. Dude is so drunk, he doesn't even look at me. Just stares at the empty space on the table.

Lola smiles a thank-you at me and eases his arm from around her waist. "I have to go too."

She's pretty. I feel sorry for her. Probably deals with stupid fucks like Rax every night. Doesn't mean she deserves to be treated like a piece of meat.

"Lola, come to the bus. Toombs and I will take you for a ride on the D-train. Twice the dick is twice as sick. Right, Toombs?"

Toombs tosses a glance toward Jinx, who's currently being eaten by the seat cushions. Ah, fuck. Poor Jinx. I gesture to the door with a quick nod, and she gets up.

"I can't go to your bus. I'm working." Lola stands, somehow avoiding Rax's slimy tentacles, and steps next to me.

"Sorry about him," I say under my breath.

"It's all right." She looks down. "I'll catch you next time you come to Jacksonville, okay?"

His bleary eyes narrow. "Next time you see me, I'll be a rich motherfucker, Lola. I'll *pay* for a night with you if you don't wanna give it to me. I'll make it rain for you in more ways than one, honey."

I wince.

"I'm sure you will." Lola smiles and walks away.

I wish I had an extra twenty to give her for putting up with Rax's obnoxious shit.

Rax hangs his head like an overly dramatic three-year-old. "There goes my woman, Toombs." He lifts an invisible glass and salutes her, then face plants on the table before them.

"You're a fuckin' cone-headed cock knocker, Rax." Toombs gets up and stretches. His shirt rides up and reveals the butt of a tattooed gun on his hip and half a six-pack of abs. A thin treasure trail of dark hair disappears down the fly of his leather pants.

Jinx and I sneak sideways peeks at each other. Shit, Toombs is ripped.

I can see the allure for Jinx, but that guy is bad fucking news. I slide my arm around her shoulder and hug her head to my neck for a second. She leans in and hugs me back. "Let's book," I say.

She nods.

"Pack it up." I point to Toombs, and we leave him to clean up Rax's mess.

"Jillian's gonna be pissed we took so long," I say as we

head for the door.

"You had sex with Shades."

I consider puking up the shot I stole from Rax just so I can spray it all over the place like they do in comedies when someone says something insane.

I stop and face Jinx. "What? No. Why would I ...? No."

"You totally did."

Blinking slowly, I touch her upper arm. "Okay, maybe that did happen once—"

"Lots more than once."

Damn. I don't give Jinx nearly enough credit. I bite my bottom lip and pray for a miracle. "Please don't tell Kate. If she finds out—"

"I won't tell," Jinx says softly. She looks away. "You know I've got a crush on Toombs, so we're even."

I worry about Jinx. I hug her. "Be careful with him. He's hiding something dark."

"Aren't we all?"

I'm not sure exactly what she means, but I kinda get where she's coming from. "He scares me a little."

"Me too. That's why I like him." Her eyes sparkle with muted fascination. I hope her curiosity doesn't lead her to take unnecessary risks.

I stretch my neck to check where Toombs and Rax are. Still at the table. "If you get involved with Toombs, you get involved with Rax by default. They come as a matched pair." I don't tell her about the one-time exception to that rule. She may already know. She's a hell of a lot more perceptive than I realized.

"I've seen how they look at each other. The way they talk. There's more to them than what's on the surface."

I could say the same about Jinx. Shit, this night is full of surprises.

"All the more reason to tread carefully. I don't want you to get hurt."

"I'm tougher than I look." She hits me with a hard stare. I believe her.

"Sorry if I get a little overprotective. I'll back off." I smile. "And by the way, you've been pounding the skins at our shows like nobody's business. Sometimes I forget to say thanks for being the best fucking drummer in the universe."

"We all rock. We don't have much of a choice." Her sweet blond pixie face and gentle voice remind me of a fragile doll sometimes. Other times, she's un-fucking-breakable. Jinx, the enigma.

We walk to the door and step into the cool, humid night air. I check my watch. It's two o'clock. Jillian's gonna hit the roof.

Where the hell did Shades go? I pull out my phone and call the queen bee.

"Where have you been, Letty?" Jillian demands.

"Sorry, we had a few drinks, talked to some people, and got thoroughly distracted."

"Get your ass over to the parking lot on Talleyrand. Now."

"We're on our way. Are Kate and Shades with you? I haven't seen them. Rax and Toombs are still inside the club."

"Nobody's here except me and Freddie. Round up the children and come home."

"Yes, Mother. We'll be there in ten." I hang up.

Great. Shades is missing.

"I'll get Rax and Toombs," Jinx says a little too eagerly.

"Okay. I'm gonna see if I can find the other two. I'll meet you at the parking lot." As soon as she's gone, I start walking and dial Shades. No answer. Now I'm getting worried.

Five minutes later, the parked bus comes into view. And I hear familiar voices outside.

"... Can't let anyone else know about this." Shades.

157

Where is he? And who's he talking to?

I dart to the shadows and home in. I tiptoe closer. He's on the other side of the bus. *Our* secret hideaway.

"Did you hear that?" Kate says.

Kate?

Silence.

"No, I didn't hear anything." Shades's voice is quieter than before, so it's harder to hear him clearly. What the hell is going on?

My stomach begins a slow descent, and my asshole puckers up. I don't like the sound of this at all.

"Take me right here. Like you did that slut in the bathroom at the strip club."

I don't believe my ears. This is not happening. What would Kate want with Shades? She loathes Killer Dixon with every ounce of concentrated hatred in her body. This must be some ploy to sabotage the tour. Kate's always thinking of herself and never about how her actions affect those around her.

"They're probably on their way back now," Shades says. "We can't risk anyone seeing us together."

I swallow hard. Oh, hell no. Hell fucking no.

"Tomorrow after the show, then," the bitch replies. "I'm sure we can find somewhere private."

No. No. Just no. I might expect this kind of sneaky behavior from Kate, but Shades? After all we've been through ... after he promised ...

He wouldn't two-time me.

Would he?

"Let's go inside before someone catches us," he says.

That slimy motherfucking traitor. Both of them.

My hands shake. My stomach rebels. My eyes tear up.

I trusted him. I had goddamn unprotected sex with him, and this is how he treats me? He tricked me into thinking I was special. That I meant something to him.

I can't believe I was naïve enough to dream I was more

than a convenient fuck.

The tears break loose and stream down my face. I shoo them away with a quick swipe and head for the door, not bothering to hide. Let them wonder whether I heard them.

A few minutes later when Shades and Kate board, he flashes me a surprised look. Yeah, pretty fucking shocking, isn't it, dick nut? I carefully engineer a neutral expression just for him.

"Where have you guys been?" I chuck the guitar magazine in my lap to the side and note their messy hair. "Did the wind get at you? Funny, I didn't notice a breeze when I came up a few minutes ago."

Kate shrugs as she passes me on her way to her bunk.

I lower my gaze down Shades's body. "You look like you've been to hell and back."

"Busy night." He lifts his studded brow like some kind of secret signal.

I snort. Yeah, I'm in on the secret. Just not the one he thinks. "What-the-fuck-ever."

Jillian wanders from the back of the bus to the lounge where we are. "Where are the rest of them? I swear, you're worse than children."

"Yeah, you just can't trust rock stars, can you?" With that comment, I give puzzled-looking Shades my back and crawl into my bunk. Fuck that asshole.

Ha, already did.

Chaos erupts when Rax, Toombs, and Jinx come in, mostly because Rax is falling-down drunk and super loud. I tug my curtain all the way to the edge and bury my head under a pillow.

Phone in hand, hoping for some kind of explanation from the guy I thought I loved, I wait for a text I never get.

INTERLEWD THREE

I can't sleep. I keep hearing Shades and Kate's conversation outside on a continuous playback. I try listening to some music on my iPod, but not even Jimi Hendrix comforts me. At some ungodly hour, I get up to pee.

As I near the bathroom, whispers and clipped movements snag my attention. In the back of the bus on the couch, Kate shuffles off Shades's lap onto the cushion beside him and sweeps a frantic hand through her hair. Shades wears the expression of a guilty-as-sin cookie thief with his chocolate-covered fingers in the jar.

I'm fucking speechless.

He stands up and runs a hand over his chest. "It's not what you think."

Feeling my face heating, I step closer. At least he has his pants on.

"Wow. For someone who claims to hate Killer Dixon with every shred of her miserable being, you sure have a funny way of showing it, Kate." Underneath my flannel pajama bottoms, my knees shake. I hitch my hands to my hips and assume an offensive pose.

Kate glares up at me through her black mess of hair.

"And you?" I say to Shades, "You're just the disappointment I pegged you to be. Entitled fucking rich boy who thinks he can buy his ticket through life. You two deserve each other."

Shades's jaw tightens. He points at Kate. "She attacked me." Anger laces his voice.

Nice try. My laugh is full of derision. Kate's is full of

disbelief.

"*I* attacked *you*?" Her lids pop open. "Motherfucker, you propositioned me outside the bus after the show and dragged me back here in hopes of screwing me while everyone was asleep!"

My heart takes off at a gallop. I'm about to lose my shit.

Shades shakes his head and steps toward me. "That's a fucking lie. Letty, I swear, it was the other way around. Come on, you know I don't give a shit about her."

"Really?" My voice trembles, and I have to wait a few seconds to reclaim control. "That's funny. I heard you two earlier behind the bus."

"Then you heard me trying to fend her off," he says.

"Don't even try that shit, Shades." Kate's cheeks redden.

"You weren't exactly firm about it," I say. "Sounded pretty noncommittal to me. But that's how you roll, right? Get it where you can. No strings attached."

Shades clasps my upper arms and gazes intently at me. "Hate to break it to you, pussycat, but your friend's a fucking liar. About everything. She lied about stealing Rax's song, and now she's trying to peg me as the bad guy when she was the one who came after me. Don't you see what she's doing? She's a pathological liar who'd love to see this tour ruined."

I break free of his hold and shove him. "Then what are you doing back here with her? Why didn't you text me?" Goddamn tears decide to build a fortress at the corners of my eyes.

"I got up for a piss. She heard me and cornered me."

"Yeah, you looked *really* cornered with her straddling you." Tear number one drops.

"When she started ranting about Rax and that song, I played along to see where she'd take it."

"That's a sorry-ass excuse. The truth is a lot less

incriminating."

"What's the matter, Letty?" Kate flashes a hateful smile. "You jealous?"

"Of you? No. If anything, I'm disappointed in myself for trusting this asshole."

Kate straightens, and her smile slides off. "Trusting him with what?" She gets up in my face. "Are you fucking him?"

I set my jaw and wipe away another droplet.

Wild light rages behind her eyes. "*You* were the one he was fucking in the bathroom at the strip club. You little cunt. Sleeping with the enemy!"

I can't believe what I'm hearing. "Uh, hello? Pot, calling Kettle. I demand you return my sooty Goth wardrobe this instant. You so much as admitted you tried to fuck him too." My voice shrills.

Something inside Kate snaps almost audibly, and the bitch unhinges. She screams a psycho battle cry in my face. Goes total fucking banshee on me. "Shades is *mine*. You'd better keep your goddamn hands off my man. I'll rip your fucking throat out while you sleep!"

The claws extend, and she comes at me. I'm in shock for a moment and can't move. Shades jumps between us, and within seconds, everyone on the bus is awake and surrounding the fray.

I've fucking had it with her shit. Before, I was devastated, gutted. Now I'm pissed.

"I don't care how good of a guitar player you are, Kate. You're a straight-up cunt." I'm totally gonna regret this, but my Piss-o-Meter is full throttle. I pull my fist back and do something I've secretly wanted to do for a while. I punch the bitch right in the face. It hurts like a motherfucker but feels so goddamn good.

Kate trips backward, her knees catch the couch, and she falls onto the leather cushions.

I shake out my hand, flex my fingers, and stomp over

to her. "You want some more o' me, bitch? I can go for days." My chest heaves.

Jillian squeezes in front of me, hands outstretched to separate us. Jinx pulls a fist to her mouth and cowers behind Toombs.

"Quiet down out there," Rax calls weakly from his bunk. Hungover motherfucker deserves whatever shit his stomach is dishing him.

Kate's eyes harden to furious black stones, all pupils and no irises. She cradles her jaw. "You just signed this band's death warrant, Letty. I'm done." I'd have laughed at her jumbled words had the message not been so devastating.

She stumbles to her feet. No one helps her. Jillian steps aside as Kate stalks down the aisle, smacking Rax's curtain along the way to her bunk. "Fuck you too, Rax. I hope you fucking die of alcohol poisoning. Or your dick rots off. Or both."

His curtain snaps open. "If it does, I'll blame your gangrenous cunt." He laughs, and then groans. "Fuck, I'm gonna puke."

I close my lids and try to calm the rage beating against my veins. I need air.

I grab my coat and exit the bus.

"Letty—" Jillian calls behind me.

"I got nothing else to say." And off I go into the night.

We're parked in a vacant lot in an unfamiliar city. I shouldn't wander the streets this late at night, but I don't know what else to do. My life lies in ruins at my feet.

Everything's gone. Everything.

Halfway to the sidewalk, I look up to the black sky. No moon tonight. No stars. I check my watch. Four a.m. December 21. It's the winter solstice. Shortest day and longest night of the whole year. The death of autumn. The day my career died.

And the death of the only love I've ever known.

"Letty." Shades's voice behind me is soft.

I shiver and turn around, keeping my focus on the ground. I want to scream at him, beat my fists against his chest, maybe twist his balls into a balloon animal. But what good would any of that do?

"I don't want to talk to you. Or anyone else," I say.

"Then let me do the talking." He steps forward and stops a few feet away from me. I can't look at him.

"Kate followed me when I left the club. On the way back to the bus, she started telling me things. She was half-lit, rambling off a bunch of paranoid, delusional shit. I tried to tune out her rant, but when she slipped up and said something about Rax's song, it got my attention. I thought it was odd she called it 'his' song and not hers after she made such a stink about it.

"So, I played along to see if she'd give up anything else. She came on to me behind the bus. Felt me up, tried to kiss me. I blew her off, but she kept at it. That must've been when you walked up."

I'm still skeptical. For a lot of reasons. "You didn't text when you got in."

"My phone went MIA. I planned to come to your bunk and tell you what happened once everyone settled, but Kate had her curtain open and was watching me like a fuckin' stalker. So, I stayed awake in bed and waited for her to fall asleep. When I thought she was out, I started for your bunk, and here she comes. I said I had to take a piss. She followed me.

"Next thing I know, she pushes me on the couch and jumps in my lap. I told her I wasn't interested. That didn't work. Then I played the 'if we get caught' card. That's when you showed up."

I want so much to believe Shades. In the darkness before dawn, pale light surrounds him. Not a halo or streetlights shining. Something else. Something vibrant. Something hopeful.

Truth hides in his voice under layers of desperation and regret.

Headlights swing in an arc, illuminating the lot. A taxi swerves toward the bus and parks beside it.

Curses and stomping feet signal Kate's descent down the steps. I pull out my phone and find Shades's number in my contacts. With my thumb hovering over the call button behind my back, I walk over to the cab. The driver pops the trunk and loads Kate's bags.

She comes up to me and points a finger in my face. "You'll regret this, Letty Dillinger."

Smiling, I hit the button on the phone and listen. Sure enough, something vibrates in the vicinity of Kate's coat pocket.

"Who's calling you at this hour?" I say.

"None of your fucking business."

Shades appears at my side. I gesture to him. "Shades says he can't find his phone. It went missing shortly after he left the club. Do you know anything about that?"

"What do you care about his phone?" Kate kicks her hip to the side.

I shrug. The vibration stops. I dial his number again, this time so she can see me. When something in her coat does a little dance, I flash the screen at her. "Funny how every time I dial *his* number, *you* vibrate. You got a rogue dildo in your pocket?"

Before she can answer, I shove my hand in and pull out Shades's cell. "Where'd you get this?"

Her face takes on a rabid tinge. "He stuck it in there to make it look like I stole it. He's a goddamn liar."

Could she be telling the truth? Could Shades have duped me?

I turn and meet his eyes. They're transparent windows into his soul. No fear. No deceit waiting to ambush me. Nothing to hide. Just pure, open honesty.

You can trust him, The Rock assures me.

After a second's debate, I take a deep breath and a leap of faith, knowing it could land me in a steaming vat of shit stew.

"No, Kate. *You're* the goddamn liar. All these years, I've taken up for you. Defended your bullshit because I thought I couldn't live without you. Well, I was half right. The band may be dead, but Letty Dillinger lives to rock another day. That's more than I can say for you. When people find out what a pathological nutjob you are, no one will ever work with you again. And believe me, I'll blab the truth to anyone who asks."

Madness lighting her face, Kate grins. "Have fun touring without a guitarist."

I nod. "I'd rather stay home than tour with a fraud like you. Good riddance, Kate."

I give Shades his phone and head for the bus steps. He grabs my hand. His arms encircle me. Todd Armstrong kisses me for two and a half eternities. The anger and pain bleed away, leaving behind squishy softness.

Two strings are strummed. One perfect harmony dances in my heart.

I shouldn't have doubted him.

Mumbling under her breath, Kate climbs gingerly into the waiting car and slams the door.

Shades is still kissing me as the taxi drives away.

When our lips part, I'm half-full and half-hollow. Half-warm, half-cold. Half-uncertain, and half-resigned.

Cherry Buzz Float is officially DOA.

I don't want to leave Shades or the tour, but my fate is sealed.

I lay my head against his strong chest and listen to his steady heart beating. "I'm gonna miss the hell out of you, Shades."

REALITY'S RUTHLESS REVELATIONS

After the dust settles from the catastrophic blowup, I spend what's left of the night in Shades's arms. I've been dying to wake up beside him since we met, and it takes the band breaking up to give me permission. Irony. Gotta fucking love it. Now that the cat's out of the bag, I feel a little lighter in some ways, but as heavy as a wrecking ball in others.

At least I got this time with him, if only one night.

He breathes softly against the back of my neck and kisses me there. The arms around my middle tighten. My guts flutter. I guess he couldn't sleep, either.

It's a curious feeling, this teetering between all-encompassing warmth and dreadful, empty cold. My heart and reality at war.

I stretch and mentally trace the lines where our bodies intersect, memorizing how we fit together so I can remember him when I'm gone. My fingers smooth the back of his rough hand.

"I'm sorry," he says. I know those two little words have a much bigger meaning than the generic apology on the surface. He's sorry I thought he was screwing Kate. He's sorry about the demise of Cherry Buzz Float. He's sorry I have to give up my dream.

"Me too." I settle into him a little while longer.

When sunlight peeks through the windows and pierces my heavy lids with its rude wake-up call, I concede it's time to get up and figure out how the hell I'm gonna get home. No point dilly-dallying.

I reach for the curtain, but Shades stops me. I turn my

head into his. Our lips almost touch.

"I don't want you to go," he says.

I smile. It's better than crying.

I roll out of bed and start cleaning up my bunk.

"Oh fuck, what have you done to me, Lola?" Rax sings into the toilet. The prick leaves the bathroom door open so we get the full effect of his stomach rebellion echoed off porcelain. Nice. Maybe leaving isn't as bad as I thought.

"You deserve that." Toombs grabs a metal support bar across the top of the bus and hangs from it. When he sees me, he says, "You skipping town or staying for the show tonight?"

"You're an insensitive cocksucker, you know that, Toombs?"

A grin splits his face into two jagged halves, neither comical. "I do my best." He saunters to the front and hops off the bus.

Jillian wanders to the coffee pot, her usually perfect hair all wonky and disheveled. She pours a cup and shakes some sugar into it. "I gotta call the venue and tell them to find another opening act for tonight." She doesn't look at me.

"Yeah."

"I hate how things went down, Letty, but maybe it's for the best." She stirs some cream into her cup and turns to me as she sips.

I cross my arms and lean against the partition. "I'm curious. How did you get Kate to agree to this tour in the first place? She was damn sure not getting on the bus until after you talked to her, and then she played the shamed puppy."

"The truth?" She sets down her coffee.

"Yeah. I'd appreciate that for once."

"I have proof that Rax really did write that goddamn song everyone's all up in arms about."

My jaw drops. "What kind of proof?"

"An email Rax sent me before the blowup. It had the lyrics along with some notes about chords and time signatures. According to Kate, she wrote it on Halloween. Rax's email dates October 2." She shrugs. "Seemed like pretty compelling evidence to me. So, I confronted Kate about it. Told her if she didn't join you on tour, I'd publicize the email."

I chuckle. "You sneaky, conniving, rat-bitch. Remind me never to get on your bad side." Wow.

"It's who I am. Look, I did it for the greater good. If I'd told you the truth, the tour would've been over before it started. You'd never have gotten a chance to shine. I wanted this for you guys." She studies her mug. "Still do. I guess it's not meant to be."

I glance out the window. Toombs strolls aimlessly around the parking lot, kicking rocks with his combat boots, head hung low. I'm tempted to join him.

Phone to his ear, Shades steps into the aisle and heads toward us. "Doesn't Cam play guitar? What about Dru? ... Shit. Okay, let me know if you find any prospects. Thanks, man." He ends his call with a heavy sigh.

"What are you up to?" Jillian asks.

He frowns. "I was looking for some chicks to audition for the open guitar spot. No luck."

My spirits lift like my miniskirt over a monitor when I hit a low G on my bass. Shades tried to save my career. I throw my arms around his neck and dive into his lips, thanking him for his efforts with a heapin' helping of tongue.

"Knock it off, you two." Jillian smacks my ass.

I ignore her and keep on keepin' on. Shades smiles around my kisses. When we break, he says, "What was that for?"

I comb my fingers through his thick, dark hair. "You tried to help Jinx and me."

171

"Yeah, but I didn't find anyone."

"Doesn't matter. It's the thought that counts."

"I've got a few more numbers in my little black book." He runs his hand up my back and raises a pierced brow. "Shower first?"

I smile. "I thought you'd never ask."

My pulse races to brand new beats as I grab a towel and follow Shades to the back.

"Uhhh ..." Rax sprawls on all fours, staring into the toilet water mirror. "Goddamn it. I'm fucking dying."

"How much did you drink last night?" Not that I'm worried. Curious more than anything.

"A bottle of vodka. Maybe two."

"Fuck, Rax. What the hell were you thinking, man?" Shades says.

"I wasn't. My dick was." He flops over on his side and rubs his stomach. "Oh, Lola ..."

Shades and I shake our heads and then follow one another into the shower.

The space is tight, but there's just enough room to bump uglies. He wastes no time parting my meat curtains with his pork sword. The water in this aqua box doesn't stay hot for long, so we double-time it by tending to washing and fuck duties simultaneously.

As soap and shampoo glide down our joined bodies, I snap my realism filter in place.

"There's a good chance this audition thing won't work out, and I'll have to leave." I meet his slow thrusts, clamoring for control of my spinning emotions, barely holding onto them.

"Yeah," he says. Another slow push into me, then retreat.

My hips urge him to move faster. He takes his time. Such a fucking tease.

Water drips into my crevices. His lunging cock wakes me from my daze, and his lips bump into mine as he says,

"There's always Athens. Meet you for drinks at BAR-k in a couple months?"

"That's all I get? A couple of lousy drinks?" I pout playfully and pretend I'm joking, but really, I'm not. "Not even a night in your dad's hotel? I'll bring the strap-on ..."

He pushes my back into the wet wall and hoists me up, impaling me in the best way. He fucks me like I'm the last woman on Earth, and I give it to him hard and heavy.

"Stay with me, Letty." Now it's not just his cock that's piercing me. His tight, intent green gaze is even sharper. It leaves a soul-deep puncture wound. "I don't have much anymore, but I'll give you everything I got."

I hug him and rock my hips into his with all the tenderness I can muster. "I don't need money to be happy. I'd love to spend the rest of the tour hanging out with you, but you know as well as I do, if I'm not making music, I'm masquerading as someone else. That's just not me, Shades."

He hits the brakes on the cock-sploration. He starts to say something but stops himself. Hope blows off his face like dandelion seeds in the wind. I lift a hand to stop them, but it's too late.

In the ensuing awkward moment, I take control of the pelvic action, but my heart's not in it. It's with those seeds that drifted away. We stare at each other in silence until our orgasms close in, give us a pair of quick, empty thrills, and leave us standing together but alone under a spray of cold water.

We towel off in silence.

Even if we do find another guitarist, no one will come close to Kate. Much as I hate to admit it, the best thing that ever happened to Cherry Buzz Float walked out of our lives a few hours ago. Kate is irreplaceable.

* * * *

"I think we need to take Rax to the hospital." Toombs's frantic pacing up and down the aisle and his pinched voice tell me something's seriously wrong. Toombs doesn't get upset about anything.

"He still puking?" Jillian asks.

"No, he's passed out. Breaths are really slow. Too slow." He rubs his hair furiously.

Jillian, Shades, Jinx, and I head to the back of the bus. Rax's still form is curled next to the toilet.

My blood pressure drops a little, and I turn to Shades. The credits roll, blaring a long list of rock 'n' roll casualties in my mind. Hendrix. Bonham. Joplin. Morrison.

"He drank a *lot* last night," I say. "He might have alcohol poisoning. We should call 911."

With no debate, Jillian whips out her phone and makes the call.

I squat next to Rax and feel his head. He's cold. Pulse is very weak. Shit, this dude is way worse off than I thought. I swallow the bile climbing my throat. If he—God forbid—dies …

Fuck. I clasp his clammy hand and hold on. Shades and Toombs hover behind me.

After the longest ten minutes of my life, a wailing ambulance rolls into the parking lot, lights blazing. The paramedics ask us to clear the bus. Toombs refuses to leave Rax's side, and I'm kinda glad. The thought of him being alone bugs me. Nobody should have to go through hell by himself. Not even a cunt monger like Rax.

As we wait outside, Shades's arms descend around me from behind, and I lean against his chest for support. He's shaking too. It's cold out here, but I'm sweating like a hog in August.

"You okay?" I say.

He stares at the bus. "Stupid prick. Why'd he have to …?" He rubs his eyes. "Shit."

I turn in his arms and lay my head on his shoulder. The pine scent of his fancy guy perfume fills my nose and comforts me a tiny bit. When he hugs me, a surge of tension releases from his muscles.

"You can't hold yourself responsible. Rax made his own choices. But he'll be okay. He has to be."

Shades must know as well as I do, I'm being overly optimistic. We should've called for help sooner. I should've recognized the signs.

But it's out of our hands now.

Two EMTs haul Rax off the bus on a stretcher. He's not moving. One of the guys holds up an IV bag. They load him into the ambulance, and Jillian flaps behind them like a clucking mother hen. "Where are you taking him? Is he gonna be okay?"

Toombs descends the steps, looking after his friend, his face a tangle of agonized lines. Jinx hangs on the sidelines, gnawing on her fingernails. Blond hair masks her face.

"Memorial Hospital," the EMT says. "You can meet us there." He closes the back of the ambulance and gets in the passenger seat. The siren screams as they peel out of the parking lot. My heart burrows into my guts.

Shades, Toombs, Jinx, Jillian, and I stand in a circle, staring at each other in a daze. How the hell did this happen? Yesterday, all was right with the world. No worries, carefree music, gigs aplenty. Today, I have no band, Rax's very life may be hanging by a thread, and everything's gone to shit.

"I'm gonna grab a taxi to the hospital." Jillian pulls out her phone and taps the screen. "Toombs, you coming with?"

The guy's face is white as snow. Lips pressed tightly

together, he shakes his head.

"Okay. I'll call you as soon as I know something. Stay put for now."

Toombs trudges to the bus. "Fucking motherfuck." He punches the side of the metal beast and climbs aboard.

Jillian disappears to the other side of the bus as she makes arrangements with the cab company. I set my jaw and meet Jinx's teary eyes. Her lips tremble, and she takes the steps, head hung.

Too overwhelmed to do anything else, I plant my ass on the pavement and rest my arms and head on bent knees. The emotion catches up with me, and I have to let it out. I can't take any more. I cry. And cry. And cry some more.

Shades drops beside me. His arms enfold me. And he holds me.

FOR THE ROCK

When I finally pull myself together, Shades follows me to the bus where it's warm. I guess it's time to pack up for real.

A beautiful, sad stream of notes pumps through a monitor. A guitar.

But both of our guitarists are out of commission. Who the hell—

Toombs?

I shiver. Goosebumps swarm my skin.

My attention poked, I head tentatively to the back of the bus, dragging Shades behind me by the hand. Jinx stands by the shower, biting her thumbnail. Toombs sits on the edge of the couch, head lowered, lids shuttered tightly, masterfully picking the strings on Rax's guitar like some kind of tribute to his friend. I knew the guy could play, but I had no idea he played like *this*. It's pure brilliance. I mean, heart gripping, deep, soulful. Not at all what I would expect from a scary dude like him.

There's way more to Toombs Badcock than meets the eye.

When the mournful song ends and I retrieve my jaw from the floor, I clap. Jinx joins my applause, and Shades smiles weakly. Maybe it's because I'm still so raw from the events of the last twenty-four hours, but I get up the nerve to lay a hand on Toombs's shoulder. "Man, that was the most beautiful fucking thing I've ever heard."

He nods once but doesn't look at me.

"How did you learn to play like that?" I sit next to him, leaving a good foot between us. Jinx slinks off to the side by the partition behind the bunks.

Toombs shrugs and breaks into another song. It's the one Rax and Kate fought over so hard. In Toombs's hands, though, it has a totally different feel. Somber notes, improvised melancholy. This guy is seriously hurting.

Fuck that.

I get up and head for my bunk trundle to get my bass. I plug the bitch in and hop on the music train with Toombs, adding in a happier groove to his tribute. He looks at me curiously but doesn't stop playing. I coax him over to the lighter side of The Rock with a funky run intermingled with exaggerated thumb slaps. Shades's palm rubs a few quick circles on my back.

Next thing I know, he's on his feet, grabbing his bass and tuning in with us. Jinx runs to her bunk for her sticks and falls in last. She doesn't have drums, but she beats the seat, the floor, the metal overhead—she makes every available surface her bitch.

It still amazes me how different she is with a pair of sticks in her hands. The coolest fucking drummer on the planet.

My personal darkness lightens as music blossoms like spring flowers around us. The mood shifts from downright depressing to hopeful. I look at the three faces surrounding me, and I let go of a laugh. Our joint musical evolution left Rax's song behind, and now it's something completely different. Jinx's head bops to a funky 5/8 beat. Shades and I duel, armed with only our basses. Toombs's expression softens as his fingers fly across the frets and his arm pumps out quirky chords.

The Rock seizes my soul, and I start rapping a bunch of shit.

"Rax's dick got him in some trouble. Shoulda stayed away from that stripper Lola. That girl brung him down to his knees. But you can't blame a stripper for being a tease. She gotta give him all she got. It's her job to get him hot.

Gotta make her some green so she can surf that stripper scene.

"Rax, why you drink so much, motherfucker? You shoot too much booze, it gonna git you, sucker. We gotcha here in our hearts, and we ain't lettin' you leave these parts. Too early for you to go, stupid fuckin' prick. You got too many more women to stuff with your dick. Think of Lola while you get better, and we'll be here singin' you musical love letters."

Shades laughs, and even Toombs cracks a smile. Jinx's blond hair flies around her head as she puts her whole body into beats she conjures like some kind of battle-hardened pixie. The music enshrouds us in a cloud of awesome, and I let it whisk me away to a happier place.

When we reach the end of our mini rock journey, the four of us look around like we're seeing each other for the first time. Toombs is no longer the scary guy I pegged him for. He's a musician. A rocker with not only a shitload of talent but a shitload of soul. We're connected. Like Jinx and Kate and I used to be. Invisible strings. I guess you can find those bastards in the places you least expect.

A collective sigh tumbles out of us, and we all chuckle uneasily. The vibe on the bus reminds me of the morning after when you're not sure whether you should ask for a phone number or get your shit and run like hell. My instinct has always been to run, but today, I think I'll stick around.

I bite my bottom lip. "That kinda fucking rocked."

Uneasy glances bandy between us. My vibrating phone interrupts the awkward silence.

I unsling my bass and answer.

It's Jillian. "They've admitted Rax. Doc says it's alcohol poisoning. They've got him on fluids, and they're pumping his stomach now. He woke up long enough to bitch about the ambulance ride, which is a good sign.

We're lucky we called when we did. If we'd waited much longer, he might've suffered permanent brain damage. Or worse."

I heave a huge sigh of relief. "Fuck, that's great news."

She exhales. "There's the matter of cancelling the gig tonight. I haven't been able to get a hold of the club yet, but I'm trying to track down the owner's home number—"

"Don't do that." Oh hell, what am I doing? Something really fucking nuts. "I mean, you can call them, but don't cancel."

Three heads lift in tandem as I make the biggest fucking foot sandwich on record. I silently beg them to forgive me while I sink my teeth into the toe cheese.

"Let us go on tonight. Me, Jinx, Shades, and Toombs. We've been practicing." Sort of. "We can play the gig—"

Toombs shakes his head and cuts off my words with his hand. "I don't play without Rax."

I palm the phone's speaker. "Tonight, you do. Just this once."

He scowls. I ignore him.

"What the hell are you talking about, Letty?" Jillian says.

"I'm talking about a merger. For one night only. Killer Dixon and Cherry Buzz Float sharing the stage in the wake of the accident. Come on, Jillian, we've got fans here. You saw them last night. They loved both bands. Don't you think they'd rather see us play together than not at all?"

Silence. All around. I don't bother looking at my bandmates. Or whatever they are.

"I don't know about this."

I don't, either. "We can totally pull it off. If we have to, we'll dish out some '70s rock covers. Everyone likes covers."

"Yeah, but who's gonna play what? You have two bassists and two drummers. That's not gonna fly."

I've got to make a sacrifice I don't want to make, but I do it. For The Rock. And for love. I want to share the stage with Shades before I leave. Just once. My farewell to this crazy, short-lived relationship that turned into the ride of a lifetime.

"Shades will play bass, Toombs on guitar, Jinx on drums, and I'll sing." I've never played a gig without my bass. Ever. But if I have to, I will tonight.

She doesn't answer.

"Please, Jillian. We'll make it work. We've already started rehearsing, and it's going great so far." Not *exactly* a lie.

"My cred is on the line here," Jillian says. "I'm trying to break out just like you are. If this backfires …"

"It won't. I swear to the Flying Spaghetti Monster, we won't let you down. Tonight, we play for Rax. And for The Rock."

Jillian sighs the way she does when she's puffing on a cig. I imagine smoke pouring out her nostrils. Will the dragon lady give us her blessing? I cross my fingers behind my back.

"Okay. I'll talk to management. There's no guarantee they'll agree, so don't get your hopes up."

I bounce on the balls of my feet. "Thank you, Jillian. Thank you for believing in me. In all of us."

"What makes you think I believe in you?"

I grin. "You didn't criticize."

"I'm biting my tongue. Prove me wrong."

"Check in when you hear something."

"Good luck." The call ends.

I face my new bandmates. "Rax's gonna be okay, but he won't be leaving the hospital until tomorrow. Looks like we'd better get to rehearsing. Jillian's gonna try to work something out with the venue for tonight."

Toombs growls through a frown. "I'm not for this shit."

"What's the matter? Afraid you can't live up to Rax's talent? Or that Jinx over there might put you to shame?"

He clenches his jaw. "Neither."

"Then what's the problem?"

His head ticks to the side, and he reaches for Rax's guitar. "No problem at all," he mumbles.

Jinx steps gingerly around him, and he eyes her with the calculation of a predator assessing his prey's fatal flaw. When she passes by, I angle toward him and whisper, "She's *so* gonna show you how it's done."

The sly hunter's expression slides into an unnerving, diabolical grin. "I look forward to it."

A hand on my ass interrupts our tête-à-tête. "Know what, pussycat?" Shades whispers behind me. He lowers the strap of my bass across my shoulders.

I absorb the twin comforts of my instrument and his tattooed arms. "What, hot cock?"

"Your lyrical bling makes my heart sing."

I laugh. "Good. 'Cause I'm fixin' to show you how to play the bass like a man, motherfucker. Think of it as Letty's last stand."

"You have no idea who you're dealing with, foxy lady."

"Oh, yes I do. You're the guy with the magic hands. And other … parts." I reach behind and tweak his dick. "Todd Armstrong, will you rock with me?"

"I'd be honored, Letty Dillinger." He brings my fingers to his lips and kisses each one. Then he drags a wrinkled bit of paper from his ass pocket and holds it before me. "How about we start with this?"

A smile spreads across my face, and I clutch the napkin to my chest. "It's about damn time you gave it back."

He leans into me and plucks the notes on my bass from the song I wrote a lifetime ago at BAR-k. The rhythm rattles the windows and brings Jinx's and Toombs's attention our way.

"You memorized it?" I say over the loud groove.

He nods and rubs his cock against my ass, nice and slow. "I figured you wrote it for me. The least I could do was learn how to play it."

My heart goes *pitter-patter.* What a fucking guy. Truth be told, even though I never got a shot at it, he plays the song better than I would have. He's got a flair for unusual improvisation. Just when I think the notes are going one way, he fakes me out and takes them in a completely different direction.

He's good. Damn good.

Toombs grafts a line of musical lightning into Shades's rhythm. I lift the strap from my shoulder, careful not to mess up Shades's fingers, and arrange it around his neck. He never misses a beat as I shimmy down.

While Shades and Toombs tinker with the notes and riffs, Jinx taps out experimental bangs, beats, and crashes on her desktop drums. The song evolves into something much bigger and better than I anticipated. I stand before our motley crew, singing and grinning from ear to ear. Shit. We're a motherfucking band.

At least for one night.

* * * *

We get the go-ahead from the venue's management and spend the rest of the day rehearsing. Between the four of us, we put together a set list of easy '70s covers pretty fast. Jinx and I pick up a few Killer Dixon songs, and Shades and Toombs learn some of ours. We manage to slap together three totally original tunes that sound pretty decent. Thank God we can all play by ear, otherwise, we'd be knee-deep in Shit Creek.

Well, we may already be there, but at least we have paddles.

Good news is, Rax is resting comfortably at the

hospital, and the doctor expects to release him first thing in the morning. They want to keep him overnight to monitor his breathing and liver functions, but Jillian says he's almost back to his old asshole self already.

I wonder if she told him about the gig tonight.

"Hey, pussycat, what do you say we grab a bite, then head in to set up?" Shades smiles, but a hint of sadness peeks through the cracks.

I'll bet my smile looks the same. Spending the day with him, Toombs, and Jinx was fucking amazing. I thought I knew what The Rock was with Cherry Buzz Float. Man, I didn't have a clue until now.

Rax will be back on his feet soon, and Killer Dixon will be whole again. Cherry Buzz Float, not so much.

But it's better to have had the experience—short-lived though it is—than to never have shared a stage at all, right?

Still, my heart aches for the possibilities within my reach that I'll never grasp.

"Yeah, I'll go with you." I put on my coat and check my wallet. Yep, still broke. "Jinx, you want food?"

She cuts a glance to Toombs, who hasn't put down Rax's guitar all day, and shakes her head. "No, I'm good."

I quirk a brow. "You sure?" I'm not wild about leaving her alone with him.

"Yep." She gives me a little thumbs-up sign.

"Okay. Call me if you need anything." I slip my last protein bar in my pocket on the way out.

Shades and I hold hands as we walk down the street. It feels so foreign, yet so natural. Like an ad for feminine hygiene products.

"So, your next stop is Gainesville," I say, making a point of focusing on the sidewalk instead of on him.

"Yeah, I guess so."

"How come you didn't freak out when your dad cut you off?" I don't know why I ask such a personal

184

question, but shit, I'll probably never see him again after tonight, so, what the hell?

He stops and faces me. "You still don't get it."

"No, I really don't."

He flashes those pearly white teeth, and a playful glint from his eyes bounces into me. "I told you. I'm lucky. Always have been. I don't let shit get me down. Look at us. Where we are. I spent twenty-six years living in luxury. Traveled the world, did things most people only dream of, but I was never satisfied. Content, yes. But not *fulfilled*.

"Then I meet you in a bar, let you do unspeakable things to me, and fell crazy-mad—" He twists his neck left and sucks his lip for a second. When his gaze swings back into mine, it almost knocks me over. "I'm a formerly loaded guy with about fifty bucks to my name. My band's in the doghouse. The tour's falling apart. And I've never been happier."

We stare at each other for a long moment. No physical touching, but damn, he's singing me a lullaby and cradling my fucking soul with that look. Bare, naked, raw. Him.

"What did you wish for when you blew out your birthday drink, Letty?" He gently pushes a strand of red from my face.

I halfheartedly snort. "I wished I could make it big with my music." I smack away a droplet that sneaks past my tear ducts. But another follows right behind, and soon, there's a whole army of them repelling down my cheeks.

He tugs me into his arms, and I fall against him. "The year's only just started. There's still plenty of time for your dream to come true."

"Maybe." I can't tell him I don't want that dream anymore if I can't share it with him.

Shit, did I really just think that? What is this, some plot by my biological clock to take my ovaries hostage? This is not me. Letty Dillinger takes no prisoners, and she certainly doesn't get sappy over guys.

Except for Todd Armstrong.

I peer up to his calm face. I want to tell him I love him. The urge to spill those cursed, radioactive beans grows stronger every hour. Maybe it's because time is running out.

"I'm leaving tomorrow. My mom's gonna wire me bus money to get home."

He nods as if he's not surprised. "I've got your number."

"Next time you're in good ol' Athens, Georgia, you give me a call. Bring dildos and plenty of lube, okay?" I try to smile through the lame joke, but regret catches my grin and twists it into a frown.

"You may not believe me, but it'll work out. Maybe not tomorrow, but soon. You'll see."

I wish I shared his certainty.

He disco twirls me out of his arms like a yo-yo, spins me back in close, and dips me within inches of the sidewalk. He leans in for a Dracula-style kiss. I laugh around his lips, despite my tears.

Tugging me to my feet, he says, "Come on. Ulysses S. Grant is burning a hole in my pocket, and I wanna buy you dinner, pussycat. You're gonna need your strength for later."

I waggle my brows. "Yeah? What do you have in mind?"

He leads me to the street corner, looks both ways, and guides me across the crosswalk. "I was thinking we should christen the stage before the gig. You know, for luck."

"What, like give it a golden shower?" My nose wrinkles.

He laughs. "Not what I had in mind. More like a Letty shower." His turn to waggle the brows.

"Suddenly, I've lost my appetite." I glance down at his fly and lick my lips. "For food."

"Nah, you need protein to keep you going. Busy night

ahead and all that jazz."

"I know exactly where to get the protein I need. But if you insist on the non-human variety, let's make this dinner thing quick. My pussy hasn't feasted on your cock in a while, and it's got a bad case of cat scratch fever at the moment."

"Letty, you move me. In the very best ways."

"I'm gonna fuck you dry and leave you with memories you'll never forget. Just be careful where you step at the show. Slippery when wet." I blow him a kiss.

"I'll be sure to put on my galoshes over the argyle socks." He straightens, and the outline of his monster boner taunts me.

I take the lead and head for the first restaurant we come upon—a sandwich joint. I reach behind me and cup his rock-hard package. Good old 'gina's got another flood in the basement.

"We're getting this shit to go."

STAGE CHRISTENING

Shades and I make quick work of our dinner and hurry back to the bus. We grab supplies, inform Jinx and Toombs we're going in to set up and work on our duet, and slip in the side door to the venue. The manager unlocked the place and said we could use the stage for practice since we're slapping shit together at the last minute. Though Shades and Toombs were able to work out a lot of their parts on the mini monitor, Jinx really needs her drums. We have a full band rehearsal in thirty minutes.

The place is mostly dark, which is fine by me. Shades leads me to the stage, and we stand in the center, looking at the empty space before us.

As horny as I am, I get a little teary-eyed. This will be a bittersweet night for sure—both the beginning and end of my dreams. I'm gonna give it all I've got, though. To the fans and to Shades.

I face him. "We're gonna tear this stage up tonight."

"Hell fuckin' yeah, pussycat. I can't wait to see you cut loose in front of the crowd." He smiles proudly and surveys the scene again. I can almost hear the screams and whistles. See the fans' excited faces.

"We'll rock this place together." I clutch the calloused fingers woven between mine.

Shades stands behind me and rubs my shoulders. The tension ebbs away, and I relax into him. His hands travel lower, down my arms, over my breasts. He hefts them, squeezes gently. His lips fall to the side of my neck and leave a trail of soft kisses. I close my lids and concentrate on feeling him—absorbing every touch and breath and heartbeat. The strings between us tangle and tighten. Instinct tells me to free myself, cut loose, move on as soon as this is done, but my heart tells me maybe it's okay to get lost every once in a while. Unraveling the knots is half the fun.

I turn in Shades's arms, and his hands wander to my butt, knead it. His kickstand presses into my belly.

"This might be the last time you get to drive the beef bus to tuna town," I say. "You'd better make it good, so I don't have any excuses to forget your hot ass."

"You won't forget me. I won't let you." His eyes sparkle in the shadows.

"Prove it."

I expect him to toss me over his shoulder like a fucking caveman, or maybe throw me face first into the wall and plow the backfield. He does something far scarier. Lips hovering a half an inch from mine, he ties me down with nothing but a stare and those unbreakable invisible strings that live to haunt and taunt me. Caught in his trap, I can't move, can't look away, can't even breathe for a few seconds. His gaze doesn't just unnerve me. It slices me open, makes me vulnerable, and puts me on display.

Thank God no one else is here to see it.

I try to fight, to wage a silent war against him, but it's no use. This prisoner is an easy target for the likes of Todd Armstrong. Such a sucker.

"I figured you out, Letty." His breath ruffles my hair. My sweat glands wake up and kick my pits with a warning injection. I'm not sure I like where this is going.

"Yeah?" My tongue is tied with him so close. I can't even think of a sassy comeback.

He nods slowly, his lips brush mine in the process. It's a goddamn miracle I don't just latch on.

"You're not afraid of anything physical, but you're

scared to death of letting your soul get too close to someone else's." His mouth barely touches mine in the sweetest, most breath-stealing kiss. No tongue. No searing passion. Just pure, naked trust delivered by a pair of love-drenched lips. My knees actually knock, elated butterflies clamor in orgiastic celebration inside my gut, and I have to hold onto Shades to keep from falling.

When the kiss ends, I can't look at him. He reads me way too well.

He tips my head up with his thumb and forces our gazes to collide. "Try this on for size. I love you."

A funny squeak slips out of my mouth, but he kisses me quiet. My lids fall shut, and I let him have me. I submit to his strong arms, his yummy woodsy scent, his strings binding me tightly.

I thought I didn't want to be tied down. I was wrong.

I surrender.

My brows twist, I try to reclaim the breath he stole, and I open my mouth to let him in. His tongue strokes mine, its metal ball teasing. We dance like that, in and out, ebb and flow, for an eternity before he pulls away and smiles.

"I knew it," he says.

I swallow. "Knew what?"

"You love me too."

"You're a delusional cocksucker." The nervous hand smoothing my hair into place must give me away. He grabs it and kisses my rough skin.

"You don't have to admit it if you're too scared, chickenshit." He takes both of my wrists and holds them behind my back. He herds me to the wall behind where Jinx's drum kit will go and presses his heat-seeking moisture missile against my cock holster, whispering against my mouth. "It's pretty obvious."

I try to wriggle free of his grip, but he's got me good and tight. So, I lick his nose. "Are we gonna fuck or what?

I don't mind putting on a show for Toombs and Jinx, but I thought you'd like to keep it just between us this last time." I doubt my false bravado is flying, but it's all I've got. I'm not into losing my shit with him. I'll do that tomorrow when I'm gone.

"Hard to get, huh?" He pushes his cock harder against me, and I spread my legs a shoulder-width apart. A rush of liquid heat funnels from my meat flaps.

"Me? No. You're the one who's hard. Now why don't you free that monster from his cage and let me see if I can tame him?" I arch a brow.

"Bet I can make you come first." He puts on a sneaky grin and releases my wrists.

"Nope. You're going down first."

"My pleasure." He licks his lips, drops his gaze to my zipper, and cups my wet cunny through my jeans.

"What do I get if I win?" I unbutton his fly, unzip, and awaken his bacon with a couple strokes.

"Your name tattooed on my Johnson." He says it with a completely straight face.

I laugh. "That would imply to future lovers that you're taken. You sure you wanna have some chick you barely know's name stuck on your dick for the rest of your life?"

He grins. "I'd be fine with that, but I'm gonna win this bet, pussycat."

I pat his cheek. "Poor boy doesn't know what he's up against."

"I've been up against you a few times. I'm fully versed in all things Letty. What's my prize when I win?"

I snort. "When. Ha! Okay, *if* you win, I'll get your name tattooed on my ass. T, asshole, D, D." I drop my pants and bend over, pointing to my bunghole. "The O will go right there, bitch."

"I'm gonna burn you so hard."

We shake on the deal, and I point to the wooden stage. "Lie down. I've got just the thing to start us off."

He follows my directions, I climb aboard the sixty-nine train, lowering my muff to his hungry lips while I get down and dirty with his man sausage. I pump my hips slowly, riding his jutting tongue, and put his cock in a headlock. The balance of devouring him while he eats me out is hypnotic. The faster he lunges into my cunt, the harder I suck him. The alternating warmth and cool of his breath mixed with the ambient air swirling in hurried rushes stands my hairs on end. The tip of his nose tickles the valley between my butt cheeks. That goddamn tongue stud coaxes mewls from my drooling mouth. I drive my hips against his face, searching for more heat, more friction, more insanity while caressing his cock between my starving lips.

We take turns moaning against each other's hot spots. I'm so glad no one else is around to hear us. We get a little crazy with the noises, and that just makes it more erotic. My pussy tightens with each lick and dive.

"Goddamn it, Shades, you make me want to squirt your fucking face," I mumble around his weeping cock. I sop up the salty droplets oozing from its head with quick tongue darts.

"Drown me, Letty." At least that's what I think he says. Hard to tell around the mouthful of pussy. His arms clamp onto my thighs and pull me in tighter against his mouth. The tongue fucking intensifies. Hard breaths from his nose hit my back door. I pucker up. Shit, I can't take much more.

I need his cum inside me—mouth, pussy, ass—I don't care where, as long as I get it. I throw a leg off and turn to face him.

He pouts. "I was just getting into that."

I squat over his engorged dick and swipe it through my cooter juice. "Get into this instead." I feed him to my cunt slowly, pausing a couple of times to adjust to his girth. God, he's so fucking big.

My clit clamors for some friction. I lean forward a tad, and ... yes. There it is. My thighs get a nice workout, doing the electric slide up and down his pole. The little man in the boat riles up and begins paddling. Shit, I may lose this bet after all. Can't have that.

I drop my chest to his and trace the borders of his lips with my tongue. His lids shut, and he smiles. I love how he gives me control. I'm doing all the thrusting now. The expression of bliss on his face tells me he's getting close.

"Are you gonna say it, Letty?"

"Say what?" I mumble against his lips. *Screw, fuck, bang* ... His eyes open and target me like a sniper. "I love you."

I look away. He's driving me mad with this talk, these words, this rising emotion. I haul myself off him and lower my lips to his dick. His knee comes up, then drops down as I suck, twirl, and devour. A hand grabs a thick mess of my hair and pulls.

"That's hardly fair." Even as he utters the words through clenched teeth, he urges my head up and down by the hair, nearly choking me with his love wand. I picture girls from our shows, screaming his name, flashing their boobs, and I smile around his dick. It might not be for long, but Shades is mine.

Now he fucks my mouth in earnest, and I fondle his balls, scraping them lightly with my fingernails, occasionally squeezing. "Fuuuck, Letty. You have the most amazing mouth."

I sit up and stroke him. "My mouth is good. My ass is even better."

The left corner of his lips curves up as I open the lube we brought and squirt it over his length. I roll to my side, lift a leg to douse myself, but his mouth barrels into my clit first. Shit, he digs in, twists, and bites. I scream. Actually *scream*.

He injects some lube in my ass, eases his index finger inside with a flick of the wrist, and dives in with his mouth on my sugared almond. Between his tongue and that driving finger, I might very well die of pleasure. Not a bad way to go.

I tighten my butt around the finger and ride. Another graze of teeth, and I clamp my legs shut, pushing him away. I can't lose this bet. It's a matter of principle. "Goddamn it, motherfucker."

Maintaining his command of my hole, he crawls behind me. My head tips back to his shoulder, and his other hand clamps my tit through my shirt. Another finger joins the one in my butt, and together they drill.

"How's that, pussycat?" His cunt-flavored lips bump mine. I dart out my tongue for a taste.

"You're a man of many talents. I'm impressed." I wiggle my ass against him and take his mouth in a long, lingering kiss. Lifting my leg, I guide his cock to my glory hole and push the fucker in as his tongue sweeps mine.

"Oh God," I groan through the lust-laced agony. His plundering kiss eases the pain. He takes me slow with a gentle push inside—just an inch or so—then retreats. Another lunge, this time a little deeper. My brow furrows. He stops, caresses my cheek.

"Again, baby," I tell him, curling an arm around his neck behind me. His gaze is pinned to mine. The sensation of being covered by his body from behind is so comforting. He pushes his cock in again, and this time, my ass opens like a fucking barn door.

"Oh my fucking Christ!" I yell. His fingers fall to my clit—probing, smearing, rubbing in slow, torturous circles. His cock in my ass is the bass line. His hand works the guitar melody that makes me sing.

Yes. I literally sing while he butt-fucks me and paddles my pink canoe. He moves me that much.

"Todd Armstrong, you pull my strings and make me sing. You tie me in knots with your balls and cock. You keep on diddling, and I'll soon be piddling. Spraying this stage with my love rage. Make me come, you gorgeous fuck bum."

His laughter beside my ear warms me. "Got my dick in your ass, an opportunity I couldn't pass," he sings back while he pumps away. "I love tweaking your clit when your legs are split. You got the sweetest cunt. The taste of her makes me grunt. Hose me down with your love mound."

Our eyes meet through the pounding, racing, and heavy breathing. I blur the line of sweat trickling down his face. "If you come with me, I'll say the words you want to hear, Shades."

He quirks his head but doesn't lose track of the beat. "Right on. That might be worth losing this bet over if you decide to fake me out at the last second."

I grind my hips up and down to the split rhythms of dick and fingers. Our music surfs the waves of my pulsing blood, skates through my veins. "No fake-outs. I'm about to blow, and I want your man chowder inside me when I do."

His adjusts his hold so his thumb rubs my nub, and he tightens his grip on my pussy. The two fingers fucking my cunt pick up speed and curl to meet the head-on pressure of the dick banging my ass on the inside. His body lunges and retreats to the complementary pump of his thrashing arm. God, he's playing me like he plays his bass. What a fucking turn-on.

Tension builds, pressure forces liquid lust upward, and the lid blows off the top, spraying clear fluid to the tune of a brain-stabbing orgasm. My legs quake, my back arches, brutal moans rattle out of me as I buck like a dying animal against the wave of Todd Armstrong. He's trying to kill me. He must be.

Teeth crash my shoulder and dig into my shirt. His deep, gritty voice grinds through my muscles and bones as he cuts his cum loose inside my ass. I milk that fucker for every last drop, and I'm still spraying twat broth. Fuck, what the hell?

I grab onto the only steady thing left in my spinning world: his lips.

He saves me with the kiss of Prince Charming scaling the walls for his princess. Jesus Johnny Christ, while my physical body whirls out of control into a vortex of pain and wonder, my heart beats steady as a Swiss clock.

Like the music I adore, Shades has a way of keeping me stable and sane. His kiss, his intense stare, and his love blaring through our private airwaves are his secret weapons.

Our arms and legs and uglies twitch through the final throes of the ass blast, but the kiss rambles on.

In this moment, I feel like I could split the cost of a lifetime with him.

Lips fall away, eyes open, and breaths slow. We stare at each other for a full minute before I make my confession. "You were right. I do love you, Shades. And not because you fucked my ass so good, I hosed the stage."

"I thought you might. I just had to prove it to you." Another kiss, and I'm officially a puddle. Literally and figuratively.

"Yo, Shades." A familiar voice from backstage ruins our moment of communion. Heavy boot falls follow.

Shades and I sit. His cock slips out of my ass. I could weep. Instead, I scramble to yank up my jeans and fasten them back together. At least we kept our clothes mostly on. Behind me, Shades reassembles himself, muttering, "Just once I'd like to fuck you without an audience."

I smile and stand.

Shit, I really did christen the stage. Vag juice dots the wooden planks underfoot. I track the droplets for a good three feet. "Damn, I've got awesome range."

"You can thank my fingers for that." He licks them and grins.

Toombs and Jinx appear in the doorway and walk over. They stop on the line of cunt splatter. I start to warn them, but nah. Serves 'em right for busting up our fun.

Shades beats me to the punch. "Watch your step. Letty spilled my drink."

Gawd.

Toombs beans us with a suspicious scowl. "Were you two planning to rehearse before the gig tonight? I don't see any instruments."

"We got a little distracted." I avoid Shades's goofy grin. He gooses my ass as I walk past. So much for keeping our "relationship" secret. Not that it was much of a secret after Kate went atomic. "I'll help Jinx set up her drums while you guys warm up."

Toombs sighs. "What the fuck were you doing?"

"Settling a bet," I reply.

"Technically, I won the bet." Shades seems rather pleased with himself. "So, when are we hitting the tattoo parlor?"

"Next time you swing through Athens."

"I'm holding you to it." He lifts a brow and says softly, "I told you I'd win."

I laugh. "Yep. You the man."

I planned to lose all along.

STRINGS

It's ten o'clock. The stage is set. Jinx and I are wearing our slut outfits. Shades and Toombs look like our pimp daddies in their ridiculous zoot suits. Nursing a sudden case of cold feet, I survey my temporary bandmates and wonder what the fuck we were thinking. Did we actually believe we could pull this shit off?

The stomping feet and chants from the roaring crowd on the other side of the world assure me our fans believe in us.

I can't let them down.

"Jinx, you ready to give your drums what for?" I play with her long blond hair.

Eyes round and face pale, she looks scared shitless, but she nods. Nervous sticks tap on her naked legs, and her breaths rush in fast whooshes. I'm not worried about her. She'll be fine. She's awesome under pressure.

Toombs, I'm not so sure about. He's pacing. Has been for an hour. Shades tried talking to him earlier, but he's not in a chatting mood. It's gotta be hard for him. This may be the first time he's ever performed without Rax. I offer him a reassuring smile, complete with devil-horn finger gestures and wagging tongue. He shakes his head at me and continues his directionless path.

Sigh. I guess there's only Shades and me left with most of our brains intact.

Who am I kidding? My brain hasn't worked right since I fucked him up the ass.

"Don't forget the key change at the bridge of 'Strings,'" I tell him. He missed it on our last run-through of that song.

Man, giving up the bass for most of this set is a hell of a sacrifice for me. Though not as much of a change as it is for Toombs. That guy is seriously talented, but I can tell by the way he eyes Jinx on her throne that he'd rather play drums.

Or maybe he'd rather play Jinx. Hard to say.

Jillian flits backstage. She's been talking to a guy for a long time. Wonder what that's about.

She lays a hand on my shoulder and dons a serious expression. "You've got the set list taped down, right?"

"Yes, Mother."

"And you'll remember the lyrics for the new songs? You screwed up 'Stun Gun' about twelve times this afternoon."

"Yes, Mother." I tap my temple. "All up here."

"I took the beer bottles off the stage and replaced them with water."

"What? I need some alcohol to loosen me up, you fucking dictator." I was looking forward to those beers. My only chance for free drinks in the near future.

Jillian shakes her head. "Nope. Not risking a replay of last night. This gig is too important."

What the hell is she going on about? "Whatever. I want beer when we're done, then."

"Give me the best gig you've ever played, and I'll buy you a keg."

"Fine, you mean old mommy."

The stomping beyond the stage increases. "Buzz, Buzz, Buzz, Buzz," the people chant.

I smile.

Shades sidles up to me. "Let's give 'em what they want, pussycat."

"Hot Letty injection. Coming right up." I stretch my neck and lay a quick kiss on his lips.

"That's my girl." He slaps my thonged ass under the

miniskirt.

Shades's girl. For one more night. I'm gonna make it the one he never forgets.

I smile at Jinx, and the two of us mount the stage. She twirls her sticks and settles behind her kit. I grab my bass from its stand and strap it on. I'll only have a few songs with my beautiful Fender baby, but it's better than none. My voice will command the spotlight tonight.

I sway up to the mic. The crowd goes nuts.

Swinging my hips back and forth, I scan the sea of bodies. The place is packed. Bare-chested guys in the front swing T-shirts around their heads. A couple of girls sit on dudes' shoulders, whistling between their fingers. The vibe is contagious. These people are here for one thing: badass music. I hope they like the Cherry Buzz Float-Killer Dixon cocktail of modern '70s rock fusion.

"Jacksonville, you're beautiful!" I shout into the microphone.

The noise intensifies.

"How many of you are here to have your dicks rocked off by Cherry Buzz Float?"

The guys whoop and holler.

"I see. I see. And how many came to flash their tits for the boys in Killer Dixon?"

The women scream. One chick in front whips off her shirt and hefts the copious contents of her bra.

I point at her. "That's dedication. I like it."

The men surrounding the flailing groupie nod appreciatively.

I adjust the mic stand and rest my foot on the monitor, giving the guys at my feet a peek at the thong underneath. One of them quirks his head at an uncomfortable-looking angle. Pervert.

"You may have heard, we had a little change of plans for tonight. Cherry Buzz Float and Killer Dixon lost their guitarists to some unfortunate series of events. They're not dead, mind you. Just otherwise occupied for the evening. So, Jinx and I, we're gonna get this party started with a treat from the rhythm section."

Jinx stomps the hi-hat pedal to a slow, steady beat. Bass drum falls in line. I nod my head in sync. My fingers join the fray and fly over the frets while my right hand thumps strings. Jinx and I cruise into our own little world of cadence and pulse, rise and fall, rock and roll. After a minute of improvised grooving, Toombs and Shades take the stage, instruments in hands, *Dorkus erectus* clothes on bodies. I keep playing and pretend to be surprised by their appearance. I shake my ass at them. The crowd's wails become deafening.

The boys walk casually over and flank me on either side. Jinx and I keep the foundations rolling, and then Toombs crashes our party with a searing guitar riff. He faces me and smiles. *Smiles.* Maybe playing guitar isn't as bad as he thought it would be.

The fans are half-shitting themselves, bouncing, screaming, moshing at our feet. I laugh at their shocked expressions.

Toombs's improv steals the show. Jinx and I fade into the background to give him center stage for a while. He closes his eyes. I feel him flowing with us in the arms of The Rock.

Kate was a great guitarist. Toombs is better.

The living, breathing mass of humanity swells as people jump, twist, and shout. Fuck, this is amazing. Shit gets totally fucking real when Shades steps behind me, leans over my shoulder and picks some notes on my bass. I lay my hands on top of his, take in the sweet flow, and we play together like we've been doing it since birth.

The heat of his chest against my back, his breath ruffling the hair next to my ear, his expert fingers guiding mine. God, this moment couldn't be more perfect. He takes control of the frets on the bass's neck, and I man the strings. I swear to fucking Christ, we share a brain. His fingers anticipate exactly where my mind is going. Every note strikes perfectly. We couldn't have done this better if we'd planned it. We are one.

This is the power of The Rock. Fusing souls. The tendrils of music twine Shades and me together, just like the strings binding our hearts.

When you think about it, strings exist everywhere. Not just between those we're connected to long term—lovers, families, friends—but also between bandmates and fans.

So, I embrace the strings while I can—the ones between Shades and me, Jinx and me, and Toombs and me. I tie myself up in them. Enjoy the feel of four minds and hearts bound into one collective ball of Rock.

As our jam session evolves, Shades slips away to launch into his own bass line, but our music and love holds us steady. The walls quake, the floor vibrates. I smile at the now-dried cum stain he and I left behind a few hours ago.

Head down, Toombs breaks into a solo that rips holes through the fabric of reality and time and space. God, imagine what living in his brain is like. Between the rhythms and melodies, it's probably a constant symphony in there.

"Guys, give it up for Toombs Badcock, strumming the six string in Rax's absence. He's fucking amazing, no?" I point to him and clap with the fans.

He keeps playing like he doesn't even notice the attention. Shades steps up while I hold court with the audience and throws down for a few measures.

I *tsk* into the mic. "I guess Shades thinks he can rock the bass better than me."

He nods to Jinx's new beat.

I face the crowd. "What do you think? Maybe we need to have a Rock Off."

"Rock off, rock off, rock off!" the people sing.

"Okay. Ladies first." I unzip my skirt and let the plaid fall around my feet. I kick the fabric aside, turn around, bare ass hanging out of my ugly red, white, and blue bikini bottom, and launch into a swirl of funk.

Pandemonium unleashes.

Shades's grin widens. Toombs and Jinx keep the tune rolling while I initiate a bass duel with Shades. We face each other, a few feet apart and stare. We don't talk. I let the music speak for me.

I love you. You rock my fucking world. This is the best day of my life.

After I finish note fishing to a huge round of applause, it's his turn. All I can think while he hits that bass with his magical fingers is, "That's my guy right there. The girls scream for him, the dudes want to be him, but I own him. Shades is *mine.*"

More applause and cheers follow his improv.

I flash him my biggest smile, then turn to the audience. "So, who wins?"

Indecipherable screams.

"How about we call it a draw?"

Shades blows me a kiss and winks as he walks away.

Appreciative whistles pierce the atmosphere as the four of us wind the song down to its conclusion. Jinx crashes her cymbal, and cheers erupt like a fucking riot.

I lift my arm in a victorious pose. I set my bass on its stand and wait for the noise level to drop a little. "Thank you so much for the warm welcome. We had to scrape some songs together at the last minute for you. Hope you don't mind a few covers."

With that, we rip into Hendrix, followed by a couple of Zeppelin tunes. When we wrap those up, it's time for "Strings." This one has a rock anthem feel. It's my favorite of the ones we wrote together because I get to sing a duet with Shades. We recycled the notes from the song I wrote on the napkin at BAR-k and added in some hooks.

> *Pull my strings*
> *Make me sing*
> *Tie me in knots*
> *You're all I've got*
> *No matter what I do*
> *I'm stuck with you*
>
> *Bound to your heart by unbreakable strings*
> *When I'm with you, my soul has wings*
> *Whichever way the pendulum swings*
> *Let's see what a life together brings*

Man, those words are harder than a dry turd in the sun to sing, knowing our future ends with this show, but I give it my best. And Shades? His eyes never leave mine through the entire tune. Our voices match in the same perfect harmony our bodies do when we make love. I had no idea being onstage with him would be so goddamn moving. So powerful. The combination of music and love takes me to a spiritual plane that exists beyond the limits of imagination.

I'm blown away.

Backed up by Toombs's haunting guitar and Jinx's steady beat, I have a hard time keeping it together. The music, the lyrics, and the longing for something bigger hold my heart captive.

I heave a sigh of relief when "Strings" ends. I was this close to bursting into tears. Ensuing whistles and cheers tell me the fans love the song as much as I do.

Thankfully, next up is a Killer Dixon tune about banging chicks. I give the mic over to Shades, pick up my bass, and stretch my fingers over the frets.

A guitar roars to life, cutting us off. I turn around. It's not Toombs. He shrugs. All four of us look left and right as the guitar hacks up the sound waves into bite-sized chunks of awesome.

A familiar face struts on to the stage, axe in hand, strumming wildly. Rax steps up to my abandoned mic.

"You can't keep a good Rax down," he shouts and pumps a fist into the air.

A huge grin spreads across Toombs's face, and Shades's jaw drops.

Not surprisingly, the audience erupts in an explosion of screams. Jillian claps from the side of the stage. She winks at me.

That crazy motherfucker. Well, this changes things. But I'm not letting a little thing like Rax Wrathbone upstage me on my last night on this tour.

I throw an arm around his shoulder. "Nice of you to join us, Rax. We've been working on a special song for you." I toss glances to the band members and mouth the word, "Lola." All three signal they get the message.

I look back at Rax. "Feel free to jump in and join us if you like." And we dive into the ridiculous tune we made up about his would-be stripper girlfriend. He laughs his way through the song, riding the improvisation wave with pompous highs and thundering lows. As in real life, Toombs follows wherever Rax goes.

Those two are like brothers, but even closer.

I swing around and stand in front of Jinx's kit. She and I are like sisters.

And Shades and me? We're lovers, bandmates, and yes, friends.

These people are my family.

I have big love for all of them. Even Rax and Toombs.

We put a lid on "Lola," and the fans clamor and shout for more. I'm having so much fun. I don't want this night to end. I hold on to it for as long as I can.

When we end our set with a mash-up homage to rock chicks Joan Jett, Heart, and Janis Joplin, I take in the scene one more time before I have to ride into the sunset.

Men and women of every size, shape, color, and age bounce on the floor at my feet. Some mosh, others hold up lights from their cell phones. People dance, scream, flounder, and laugh.

They are the reason I play music. They're my motivation for getting out of bed in the morning. They're why I don't get a respectable job that pays decent money. I don't want to be respectable or rich. I want to rock. I want to sing my heart out to fans every night.

I want to be this chick—the one I am right now—for the rest of my life.

As the last drum rolls and the cymbal crash signals the final downbeat of both our song and our short-lived career as a chicks-and-dicks fusion group, I'm thankful to have had the opportunity to play with these amazing dudes.

Heart in my throat, I smile at Shades and salute him.

"Thank you for the pleasure of your company, Jacksonville. Good night!" I yell into the mic. I rush from the stage before I lose my shit. Concern etched in deep lines around his eyes, Shades watches me rush past.

Jillian snatches me in her arms before I can get away. The bitch *hugs* me.

My first instinct is to push her off because any kind of affection from her is so unexpected. But I let her squeeze me for a few seconds. The shock holds my tears at bay.

"What got into you?" I say when she lets go.

And she's grinning too. What the fuck? "You did me right, that's what got into me. That was fucking amazing, Letty."

A frown sneaks across my face against my will. I try to transpose it into a smile, but my cheek muscles are having some trouble remaining steady. Trapped between Jillian and the band exiting the stage, I'm stuck.

Heat warms my back, a sweaty head falls to my

shoulder, and a pair of big hands drape around my waist. "Have I ever told you how much I love your voice?" Shades says.

"No."

"And your bass playing."

"No."

"And your ass cheeks." He pinches one.

"Maybe indirectly."

"You gonna hog her all for yourself, asshole?" Rax steps around front and center, wedging between Jillian and me.

"Yeah. I decided I'm not into sharing." Shades tightens his grip on me. I lean into him and absorb the warmth.

Rax rakes his gaze down my front to the thong I just realized I'm still wearing. "Well, if you ever change your mind, Squirt ..."

"You're such a douche, Rax."

"Glad you're still kicking, man." Toombs reaches between us and smacks Rax's open hand. Shades joins in the macho display.

"You know me," Rax brags. "I'd never let dumb shit like alcohol poisoning get in the way of a gig."

"If you want me to be your manager, you'll never binge drink like that again, you stupid twat," Jillian says.

I know Jillian meant nothing by the comment, but it slices my guts wide open. She'll stay with the guys on tour. Which means even if Jinx and I find a replacement for Kate, we'll be without a manager. Shit, I hadn't even thought about what else would be affected by the band's breakup.

"I won't be drinking anything for a while." Rax rubs his stomach. "But I do want to go back to the strip club and see if Lola's still there. That chick was so fucking hot. I'd love to break her heart."

Great. So, I guess it's back to business as usual for the guys. Like Jinx and I never happened. Whatever.

I snag my drummer's eye and wave her over from the corner. Doused in a sheen of sweat, Jinx shyly joins me. "You outdid yourself tonight," I tell her. "I'm proud to know you, wild pixie."

"Same here." With a forced grin, she watches the interactions among the guys. I share her jealous longing. Wishing for things that can't be.

Standing in the aftermath of achieving my dreams only to have them returned for being too big, I turn to Shades. "I'm gonna help Jinx load her drums, and then we'll head back to the bus. You guys go off and have fun. I'll catch you later."

"I'm not going anywhere without you, pussycat."

"You have celebrating to do. Go on. I'll be there when you're done." Maybe.

"Can I have a word with you, Jillian?" The guy Jillian spoke with before the show joins the circle. He flashes a curt smile to the rest of us.

Jillian straightens. "Absolutely. Nobody leave." She points at me. "I'll be right back."

Rax and Toombs are having a "reunited" moment. I feel awkward standing here while they talk about what happened at the hospital and how Rax's gonna change his ways so there won't be any more setbacks on the tour. I'm pretty sure Jinx is as uncomfortable as I am.

And Shades? He just stares at me. I can't tell what's on his mind. Is he sad that I'm leaving? He told me he loved me. You'd think he'd be upset if that were the case. Maybe he's plotting his next female takeover. Done with me, so he can move on to someone new.

Well, if I have to, I can move on too. I don't need him or anyone else to validate me as a musician or a woman. I'm Letty Dillinger with or without him. There are plenty of other dudes out there to bang. I can switch off my pesky emotional circuitry in the blink of an eye and forget I ever met Shades.

I *can.*

I just don't want to.

"What are you looking at?" I'm afraid to ask.

He licks his lips. "The hottest piece of ass I've ever had."

Jinx arches a brow and slips into the shadows by the wall. The tension between us loosens, along with the constriction in my bronchial passageways. "You say the nicest things."

He pulls me into a hug and rests his cheek on the top of my head. "Your ass is amazing, but my favorite part is your voice. It's raspy and kinda deep. Like aged whiskey and battery acid splattered across a wall of graffiti. So fucking sexy, Letty."

I laugh. Maybe blush a little.

His hard stare pins me like a bug in a collection. "It's gonna take you places."

"It's taking me away from you." Well, not my voice per se, but my inability to use it with his band in the vicinity. Ah, shit, I shouldn't bring him down with reality after this awesome gig.

"You and I sang a duet about things that tie us together." He presses a hand to my chest. At first, I assume he's feeling me up through the bikini top, but then I realize he's not after a tit grope. He's going for my heart. "We got something that binds us, no matter where we are. Together or apart, close or far."

Why'd he have to go and say that?

Jillian returns and gestures to the guy behind her. "This is Rick Johnson. He's an executive at Megaphonia Music & Entertainment in Hollywood." Her eyes flash big green dollar signs.

What the—

"I gotta tell you, I loved what you did onstage tonight." Johnson looks at each one of us in turn. "I'd like to talk to you about your future in music."

SLAP MY BARE ASS AND CALL ME SASSY

It takes me a couple minutes to peel my tongue off the floor and roll it back into my mouth, but eventually I do. Jinx curls into my arms, drumsticks and all. I hug her as she leaks tears down my star-spangled boobs, which are already streaked with a few wet stripes of my own. Seems I have a problem keeping my emotions on a leash too. Especially when Shades's tattoos cover my bare belly from behind, and his stubble grates my cheek.

Rax joins us from the side. And fuck me, Toombs squeezes awkwardly into our huddle, though I'm pretty sure he's just using it as an excuse to goose Jinx.

When Jillian piles in, shit gets real. A wild hair tickles my fancy. I motion for the guys to help me. We lift our squealing, writhing bitch manager above our heads while Mr. Record Executive looks on with a guarded smile.

"Jillian, Jillian, Jillian," we chant.

"Put me down, you assholes." Jillian pretends like she's mad, but her giggles give her away. She's kinda cute when she lets her guard down.

We set her on her feet, and suddenly, I'm very self-conscious in my slut bikini and thong. I back into Shades and lay my arms on top of his.

"Told you everything would work out, Lucky Letty," he whispers into my hair. "You should listen to me more often."

"Let's hear what he has to say before we get too ahead of ourselves." But I know as well as he does he was right all along. I didn't trust in The Rock—or our strings—as I should have.

He takes off his disgusting pinstripe jacket and tosses it around my shoulders, then resumes his position behind me. The coat smells like Shades—pine and musk and hot, sweaty man who's gonna get the fucking of his life in a couple hours. God, honey's already dripping down the inside of my thigh from just thinking about it.

I turn to Jillian. "Why didn't you tell us who he was?" I nod to Mr. Johnson.

She scoffs. "No way in hell I was telling anyone anything. If you'd known, you'd have made a mess of things for sure. You guys didn't need the pressure with everything else going on." She pauses and glances at Rax. "And you showing up when you did worked out perfectly. How did you get out of the hospital, anyway?"

Rax grins slyly. "Made a deal with one of the nurses. Said I'd give her the orgasm of a lifetime if she let me go."

Toombs snaps his gaze to Rax. "So, it went well."

"Don't know. She's supposed to meet us at the bus in fifteen. Maybe she'll bring friends." Rax shrugs.

Toombs tenses. He steps away from the group to the side of the room farthest from Jinx.

I'm still not sure what's up with the Rax-Toombs two-for-one prize package, but I hope Jinx doesn't get in the middle of it. I pull her over and sling an arm around her.

"Can we get back to business, children?" Jillian's voice gets snappy. "We have a lot to negotiate, but the short of it is, Megaphonia wants to sign you."

Johnson steps up and raises a finger. "As a five-piece. I've heard the music from your respective bands, and it's good. But the show you put on tonight was epic. I don't know what you did or how you did it, but the blend of the two bands is bigger and better than your separate sounds. You have just the 'It Factor' I've been looking for—the perfect blend of modern music with '70s soul. Great hooks, great voice, great beats. And having two massive fan bases doesn't hurt. Only thing you have to do now is

212

write an album together and come up with a name for the new band."

"What's wrong with Killer Dixon?" Rax demands.

I turn on him. "What's wrong with Cherry Buzz Float?"

"That's a stupid girly name."

"And you're a cocksucker. Your point?"

Jillian holds her hands between us. "Okay, kids. No more fighting. We've had quite enough of that. We'll think of a brand-new name that everyone agrees on, *capisce*?" She faces Johnson. "They're really not normally this bad."

I love how Jillian lies for us. It's touching.

The guy shrugs. "Truth is, I don't care if you get along or not. Do whatever you gotta do to figure out your process. Group dynamics don't concern me. I'm only interested in making money for Megaphonia."

Well, at least he's honest. I can respect that.

"We'll make you plenty of money," Rax says.

Johnson meets his eyes. "I hope so." He pauses and then looks at Jillian. "I've got an early morning, so I'm gonna shove off. I'll email you details tomorrow, and we'll set up a meeting in LA with the other executives."

"Sounds great," she says and walks him to the door.

The stage crew brings in pieces of Jinx's drum kit and loads them into cases.

Johnson lays a hand on the knob and turns to us. "Congratulations. I'll be in touch."

"Thanks," I say as he and Jillian disappear into the darkness.

"Holy fuckin' shit." Rax's grin might as well go ahead and eat the rest of his face. It's halfway there. He slaps Toombs's hand, then Shades's. "We finally made it."

"Yeah, with a little help from two badass chicks," I add, high-fiving Jinx.

Rax snorts. "Chicks are only good for two things: banging and ... I don't know what else."

"Rocking your fucking nuts off." I punch Rax's shoulder.

"All right, all right. You *may* have a point, Squirt."

"The next time you call me that, I'll skewer your nuts with Jinx's drumstick and feed 'em to you. Raw." I drill him with a hard stare and cut my eyes to Toombs, hoping Rax picks up on the underlying threat. Now that I don't have to worry about Kate, I have no qualms about spilling the details of our night together.

Rax holds up his hands in surrender. "Okay, if I can't call you Squirt, how about we name the band The Squirts?"

"What, so people can say we're a load of shit?" Shades says. "Let's not give anyone unnecessary ammunition."

"How about Killer Buzz Float?" Jinx's voice is so soft, I almost miss what she says.

All movement in the room stops. Curious, thoughtful glances pinball between us.

"Killer Buzz Float," Toombs says as if taking the name for a test drive to see if he likes it.

Rax nods slowly. Shades half-smiles.

"It's appropriately stupid, and blends our two band names well," I say. "Our existing fans will appreciate it. I vote yes."

"I'm in." Toombs stares at Jinx, who bites her fingernail.

"It'll do," Rax says.

"Hell yeah," Shades chimes in.

Jinx straightens and smiles a little. "Killer Buzz Float it is."

Toombs lifts his hand to her, and she slaps it gently. An explosion of smacks follow as the rest of us get in on the action.

"We should celebrate," Rax says.

"Round of drinks?" Shades asks. "You buying?"

I love that he's as broke as I am and begging booze off

his friends.

Rax rubs his stomach. "If I never see another bottle of liquor in my life, it'll be too soon. I was thinking more like hitting the strip club."

"You said you had a nurse waiting for you on the bus," I remind him.

"Fuck her." Rax scowls.

"I thought that was the point."

"No, I want me some rack of Lola tonight. Toombs, you with me?"

The drummer-turned-badass-guitarist sneaks a peek at Jinx, who buries her attention in a spot on the floor. "Yeah, I guess," he says.

Jinx's face scrunches a little under the curtain of her hair. Damn it. She really does like Toombs.

Something's gonna have to give between Rax and Toombs. I can see them both heading in opposite directions, and I sure as shit don't want to live through another band blowup like we had with Kate.

Fucking Kate. Good riddance, bitch. She got what was coming to her: nothing.

"I guess everyone's going their own way, then?" Jillian says as she walks over.

"You're welcome to come to the club with me and Toombs." Rax slaps Toombs on the shoulder.

Jillian's eyes narrow. "I could go for some tits and ass. I'm in."

Five jaws drop with a collective creak.

No. Jillian's not—

No way.

"You're a muff muncher, J? Really?"

She laughs and shrugs. "You didn't think it was odd that I live by myself in the middle of nowhere, never hang around with guys aside from these dickheads," she swats Rax's ass, "and I love hockey? Come on."

"I think I'm in love." Rax grabs Jillian around the waist

and spins her. "Let's go, bitch."

"I'm coming too," Jinx says.

Way to go, Jinx. I flash her a secret smile. Even better, Toombs stares at her like a starving man before his last meal. Now, if he could just get rid of Rax for a while. Maybe Lola will be a good distraction. I cross my fingers for Jinx.

Jillian waves a hand at the equipment. "Leave your stuff here. Management said we can pick it up in the morning when we settle our bill."

Bill? Maybe that means we'll finally get some money we don't have to spend on diesel or food. Fuck, my life just got real. In so many ways.

I squeeze Shades's hand. "We'll meet you guys at the club. I need to go back to the bus and change."

Jinx nods at me and covers a smile as she follows Toombs, Rax, and Jillian out the door.

I turn to Shades. Beautiful Shades. He's still wearing his sunglasses from the gig. I snatch them off. "I guess you're pretty pleased with yourself, huh, handsome?"

"Why's that?" His grin primes my nubbin for an explosion. The Letty tap is open for business. With him around, when is it not?

"I get the feeling you like proving me wrong."

He touches my hair, and I nuzzle his palm. His face is flushed, his shirt still a little damp from playing. He stares at me. I could stand here with him, basking in this moment forever.

"No. I like proving you right," he says.

I drown in the green pools of his eyes. "No idea what you mean by that, but okay." It could be I'm suffering from interference in frontal brain function. Oddly, ninety percent of the shutdown is due to the Shades factor, and not the record deal of a lifetime. Go fucking figure.

He nudges a knee between my legs and inches closer. "You never stopped believing in yourself when you had every reason to quit. You stood up to overwhelming odds and beat the shit out of the system using your biggest, strongest weapon: your voice. You thought you didn't have it in you, but I knew you did. I never doubted you, Letty. I never doubted us."

I stare into those penetrating emeralds and let go of the emotion. Because what can you say to faith like that? Not a goddamn thing.

"Fuck you, Todd Armstrong, for making me cry." I swipe at the tears. He guides me to his chest. "How come I never cried until I met you? You have some kind of emotional disruptor beam embedded in your cock? Should I notify the government? I gotta know if I'm inadvertently harboring a secret weapon in my furburger when we have sex. In case of misfire or—"

He cuts off my rambling rant with a kiss that doesn't turn me on. It drags me kicking and screaming to the heights of Mt. Lovemore where lust is an afterthought and the invisible strings of separate lifetimes weave together a new tapestry of perfect, unbreakable knots. This kiss shapes the future of our lives together. This kiss dares me to try *thinking* about anyone else.

When his tongue makes a slow, agonizing retreat, our lips part, and my eyes flutter open. Shades is gone. Some other guy stands above me, arms strong around my back, just like his namesake. Todd Armstrong loves me.

"I love you too." I'm breathless and sweaty, despite the cold and the bikini. He's warm and hard, and hotter than a porn queen at a Boy Scouts reunion, despite the ridiculous suit. "And my monkey is jonesing for a Shades-flavored banana."

He reaches in his nasty pants pocket and pulls out a wad of dollar bills. "Quickie on the bus, then off to celebrate with *our* band afterward? I have thirty-two bucks left, pussycat. They're all yours."

"Keep your money. Never know when you might get a

hankerin' for another dildo."

"With you in the driver's seat, there's no telling where this ride's taking us."

I pause on our way to the door. "So, you're not opposed to another leisurely stroll up the Hershey Highway? Be still my beating heart."

He stops me, spreads open the coat wide enough to cover what he's doing. He wiggles a finger over the lip of my bikini bottom and plunges it into my slick pussy. I gasp, and my chest heaves under the influence of surging adrenaline.

Leaning close enough for me to count his whiskers, he mines my vag for oil and says softly, "You do what you gotta do, and so will I. We're heading to the bus. When we get there, I need you humping my face. Breathing is optional. Orgasms are mandatory. You don't leave until you squirt at least twice. Understand?"

I try in vain to catch my breath. "We may be in for a long night."

The corner of his mouth twitches into a smile, and he slows his strokes. "I hope so."

I rest my arms on his shoulders and press my clit against his palm. Two of his fingers lodge deep inside me. The friction of their calculated movement lures more juice from the factory. "Shades?" I breathe his name like a breeze against his ear.

He turns his lips into mine, presses his forehead to my wet hair, and gazes at me like a cunning lion. "Letty?"

"I think we should make a pact to christen every stage Killer Buzz Float plays on. For luck."

"Damn, girl. You move me. You got yourself a deal." He tweaks my clit with his thumb and pulls out. "But you don't need luck. I got plenty for the both of us."

I assume command of his pussy-spit covered hand and walk him the rest of the way to the door, smearing the sticky goo between his fingers. "Okay, for down-and-dirty love, then."

"Is there any other kind?"

I pause to think about it. "Nope." God, imagine all the possibilities—all the knots we can tie in these strings of ours.

Being entangled in music, sex, and love never felt so good.

CODAS, VOWS, AND DATA PLANS

"Five, four, three, two, one ... Happy New Year!" Everyone in the Miami bar jumps to their feet as the apple drops to the bottom of the television screen. I spin to face Shades and throw my arms around his broad shoulders. He grins and lays a searing kiss on my mouth.

Laughter and cheers bloom around us. Patrons sing "Auld Lang Syne." Bodies sway left and right. Arms raise. It's kind of like a Killer Buzz Float show.

"Happy New Year, pussycat." Shades smooths my hair.

I raise my shot glass. "To music, love, and cell phones."

"To new beginnings." He clinks his tequila shooter to mine, and we throw our liquor back at the same time.

"I need another photo. Our first one of the year." I pull out my brand-spanking-new smartphone and wave it proudly.

Shades rolls his eyes. "Not another one. You've taken at least a hundred pictures of me today."

"This one is of *us*." I sling an arm around him and point the camera at our happy faces. "Say 'cooter juice.'"

"Cooter juice."

Snap.

"One more."

He sighs and puts on another smile for me. This pic is even better. "Perfect."

I scroll through the images. My phone is so fucking awesome. I can take pictures. I can email. I can text. Social networking, music, even books and movies—they're all here in this tiny little device. God, it's a marvel.

Shades is thoroughly unimpressed. I shake my head. It's gonna take a while for me to beat the rich out of him, but I'm working on it. He took his first step on the road to recovery by letting me buy the drinks tonight. Now that he's as poor as I am, we're struggling musicians together. Do you have any idea how much fun it is being broke with someone you love? Tons!

Though, thanks to our new record deal, for the first time in my adult life, I have a *little* spending money. Hence the kickass phone. It's my only vice.

I smile as I log in to Killer Buzz Float's new fan page and post the pic of Shades and me.

He watches over my shoulder as I type: *Happy New Year from Shades and Letty. Looking forward to rocking Miami tomorrow night.*

Three likes pop up on the status update before I log out. It sure is nice to feel loved. By fans and by Shades.

I nudge his shoulder and kiss his stubbly cheek. A random memory from several weeks ago invades my brain. "Hey, remember that bet we made at Jillian's house about the stripping video? After Kate left, I never bothered comparing Cherry Buzz Float's page with Killer Dixon's. I wonder which band got the most likes?"

Jinx and I have moved on from CBF and all the shit with Kate. It's easy to forget some songs once you hit the coda. But pride makes me want to know who won the bet.

Shades takes out his phone. "Let's find out." He taps in the web address as Rax, Toombs, Jillian, and Jinx approach the table.

Toombs and Jinx stand close, but they don't touch. They never do. Yet, there's electricity between them. They won't look at each other during rehearsal, and Jinx gets territorial every time Toombs encroaches on her drum space. But away from the music, they can't keep their eyes off each other. Hot and cold, those two. I can't figure them out.

Rax, on the other hand, is the same old wanker he's always been except for his incessant pining for that Lola chick from the strip club. It's been almost two weeks since he saw her, but he's still yakking about how pretty she is and how he could change for a woman like her.

Right. Guys like Rax don't change. They just grow up to be wrinkly old letches who perv through binoculars on hot, young joggers as their asses bounce down the street. At least his obsession with Lola takes some of his focus off me.

"Where have you guys been?" I say.

"Scoping the crowd for chicks to bang. No luck." There's no zest in Rax's voice. I'm starting to wonder if Lola really whipped him.

"Well, how about we all pose for a picture?"

A collective grunt rises from the group.

"Come on. I need something to fill my blank home screen." I wave my bandmates closer.

They grudgingly come together. I shove my phone into Jillian's hands. "You're in charge."

"Well, duh." She shakes her head and points the camera at us. "Pretend like you love each other."

I grope Jinx's boob, and she falls out giggling. Shades's hand thwacks my butt. I squeal like a pig. Rax and Toombs make silly kissy faces at each other. Jillian snaps the picture.

We gather around the phone to take a look. The four people who turned my life around smile up at me from my first real present to myself. It's fucking perfect.

I look at each of my friends in turn. "Thanks, dudes. For everything."

Hand slaps and hugs ensue. Before I have a chance to go all "I love you guys!" on everyone, Shades laughs at something on his phone and lifts a fist in triumph.

"I knew it," he says.

"What?"

He grins at me. "Killer Dixon won the bet. We had two hundred and thirty-nine more likes than you did."

"What? You've gotta be shitting me. That's so unfair."

"Yeah, you had almost a thousand more than we did before we even made that bet," Jinx says. It's the most I've heard out of her mouth in, like, ever.

"Still, a bet's a bet." Rax licks his lips. "You're not gonna renege, are you?"

Shades lifts his pierced brow. Toombs cuts his eyes to Jinx.

"As arbiter of said bet," Jillian interrupts, "I think it's only fair that the remaining members of Cherry Buzz Float uphold their end of the deal."

I crack our manager with a glare. "You just want to see tits. You don't have to publicly humiliate me for that. I'll show 'em to you any time."

She half-shrugs.

I take a deep breath and face my drummer and best girl friend. "What do you say, Jinx? We did vow to let them video us giving them lap dances."

She presses her lips together. "Fair's fair."

I love this bold new Jinx.

I point a thumb toward the bartender. "Somebody go ask if they have any Zeppelin. And find me a pole in this place."

Toombs bolts toward the bar like a dying man in need of a shot. Rax's smug grin crawls under my skin. And then there's my other best friend, Shades. All smiles.

"Me first," he says.

I slide my leg across his thigh and straddle him. I flip up his sunglasses and plant a soft kiss on his lips. "You only. Jinx can handle Toombs and Rax," I say loud enough for her to hear.

"Uh ..." She shoots a desperate, pleading look my way.

"And what about me? As your manager, I'm supposed to get twenty percent of everything." Jillian waves her electronic cigarette.

"Twenty? I thought it was fifteen?"

"I upped my fee."

I harrumph. "You get to video with my new phone." I pass my baby back to her and press my tits into Shades's face.

I swipe his cheek. "Are your strings ready to be plucked?"

"By you? All day, every day. Pour some Letty on me." Ah, my beautiful Shades.

The music cranks loud. Bartender holds up a thumb. Excitement steeps the atmosphere. I slide off Shades's lap and mount the table. All heads turn my way.

"Good evening, Miami," I yell to the crowd. "My name is Letty Dillinger, and I was born to rock your motherfucking face off."

Cheers erupt, claps punctuate the air, and I turn the entire place upside down with a lap dance on Shades's rigid cock that would make Mata Hari's toes curl with envy.

The song ends, applause deafens, and Shades stares into my eyes with such pure devotion, my heart misses a beat. Amid the laughter and shouts, I lean forward and say in his ear, "You have a massive erection."

He grins. "I was worried you wouldn't notice."

I glance down. "Hard not to notice a cock like yours. What do you say we blow this joint and troll the streets for a twenty-four-hour adult toy store? Hell, maybe we could engage in a little public indecency on the beach. On a night like this, I'll bet no one would bat an eyelash."

"Hell's bells, pussycat. I'm all yours."

"Yeah, you are. Don't you ever fucking forget it." I kiss the words into him so he won't.

Twenty-five years ago, I entered this world kicking and screaming. If I have my way—and The Rock willing—I'll keep it up till the day I die. With an awesome family and an amazing, supportive man like mine, hell-raising is an afterthought, rocking crowds is easier than breathing, and loving both Shades and *myself* is effortless.

My name is Letty Dillinger, and I'm a fucking star.

ACKNOWLEDGMENTS

Thanks to Amy Queau for the beautiful new cover; Noelle Pierce for early feedback and sprints at Starbucks; Emma Smith for the list of hilarious sexual euphemisms; Jenn Sommersby Young for stellar editorial guidance, patience, and friendship; Maya Lynn Watson for brainstorming the awesome series title, "Hard Rock Harlots"; and my readers for keeping me motivated with kind words and unwavering support.

As always, big love goes to my friends and family for putting up with my riotous shenanigans, foul mouth, and filthy mind.

ABOUT THE AUTHOR

A whale warrior, indie freedom fighter, and vodka martini aficionado, Kendall Grey is calm like an F-bomb*. She writes about fierce women and the men who love them.

Kendall lives off a dirt road near Atlanta, Georgia, with three mischievous Demonlings, a dashing geek in cyber armor, a long-haired miniature Dachshund that thinks she's a cat, and an Aussie shepherd mix whose ice-blue eyes will steal your heart and hold it for ransom.

*Detonation manual not included.

kendallgrey.com
Newsletter: bit.ly/HardRockHarlotsNewsletter
facebook.com/KendallGreyAuthor
twitter.com/kendallgrey1
instagram.com/kendallgrey1

ALSO BY KENDALL GREY

Alpha Prez and the First Lady's Secret Weapon

Ghosts

Hard Rock Harlots Series

Strings
Beats
Nocturnes
Rock
Bang

Just Breathe Series

Inhale
Exhale
Just Breathe

'Ohana Series

Hot-Blooded